"I've been kidnapped,"

Sandra said breathlessly into the cell phone.

"What?" her friend Belle gasped.

"Everything was fine until a few minutes ago," Sandra whispered. "Now my fortune is gone, and I've been kidnapped."

"Where are you?" Belle asked.

"In a stretch limo."

"This sounds like a rather pleasant kidnapping," Belle said dryly.

"And you should see my kidnapper." Sandra sighed. "He has the face of a movie star, a hot bod and the most gorgeous pair of violet eyes...."

"Just give me your location—" The phone suddenly went dead.

Through the glass Sandra's kidnapper shook his head. Somehow he'd cut off their call.

In a fit of frustration, Sandra banged on the partition. If only she had called 911 instead of going *on* and *on* about her hunky kidnapper....

Dear Reader,

Going Overboard. Sandra and the Scoundrel. I think the titles of this month's LOVE & LAUGHTER books explain themselves and the appeal of romantic comedy. After all, what's better than experiencing opposites finding romance and humor!

Spectacular Vicki Lewis Thompson continues her winning stories with *Going Overboard,* otherwise known as the houseboat cruise from hell. Ever the adventurer, Vicki undertook her own houseboat trip and, as a result, has firsthand experience of many of the mishaps found in the novel. Since then, Vicki's become a real land lover.

Always funny Jacqueline Diamond pens her second LOVE & LAUGHTER romance about a secondary character from *Punchline.* Sandra Duval is everything a flighty heiress should be (including owning and wearing an outrageous collection of bizarre hats and costumes) and completely lovable as she is confronted with the complete unknown: children!

So, have a laugh on us and enjoy the romance!

Malle Vallik

Malle Vallik
Associate Senior Editor

SANDRA AND THE SCOUNDREL
Jacqueline Diamond

Harlequin Books

TORONTO • NEW YORK • LONDON
AMSTERDAM • PARIS • SYDNEY • HAMBURG
STOCKHOLM • ATHENS • TOKYO • MILAN
MADRID • WARSAW • BUDAPEST • AUCKLAND

ISBN 0-373-44032-4

SANDRA AND THE SCOUNDREL

Copyright © 1997 by Jackie Hyman

This edition published by arrangement with Harlequin Books S.A.

Printed in U.S.A.

A funny thing happened...

Unlike the children in this book, my two boys never believed that dancing and drinking ginger ale would make grown-ups fall in love. But they've had plenty of strange notions of their own.

My favorite unanswerable question was, "Mom, why is the universe in outer space?"

Another time, I switched gears on my younger son, then age four, and began plying *him* with questions. When I got to "Why do we wear clothes?" he answered without hesitation, "So people won't laugh."

—Jacqueline Diamond

To Kathryn Brockman and Gumbo

1

It was on her thirty-second birthday that Sandra Duval discovered she no longer lived a charmed life.

To start with, eighty-year-old Mrs. Octavia Smith wore a much more striking hat to a charity breakfast. Bedecked with real orchids, real calla lilies and a realistic-looking stuffed monkey, the hat rode rakishly atop the dowager's champagne-dyed curls.

Her own white silk chapeau trimmed with miniature trellises, red silk roses and a shepherdess doll was sedate in comparison, which made Sandra feel *completely* overshadowed.

Then, later, at a luncheon for supporters of the Los Angeles Music Center, the mayor shook hands with the ambassador from Tonga and a boy soprano before he even noticed Sandra.

She was not accustomed to such cavalier treatment. After all, she had been a major contributor to the music center. Her husband had died seven years earlier and left her an inheritance of fifty million dollars. She had donated millions to the center, and she certainly deserved better than this.

Sandra had no inkling, however, that the worst was yet to come. After the luncheon she emerged from the music center into the June sunshine with her rose-trimmed hat on straight and a confident smile decorating her lips.

She didn't suspect the cluster of reporters and photographers on the sidewalk of anything more than their usual idle curiosity—even when, after sighting her, they blocked the path to her limousine. The press, after all, often accosted her when they had nothing better to do.

"Mrs. Duval!" called one of the female reporters. "How do you feel about losing all your money?"

"Excuse me?" Sandra couldn't understand why people insisted on asking hypothetical questions. She had a very literal mind, particularly where money was concerned.

"Do you believe your lawyer really committed suicide after stealing it, or do you think he may have faked his death?" a male reporter boomed out.

"Suicide? My lawyer?" Her hands fluttered helplessly. It was a gesture her late husband had found irresistible, and she still employed it when distressed. But the cause of her distress was usually inconsequential and mild in nature, and had nothing to do with embezzling lawyers committing suicide.

Why hadn't her personal assistant briefed her? What *was* going on here?

"What are you doing to find the money?"

She couldn't see who was talking, not with so many lights flashing in her face.

"What about the foreclosure on your mansion? Where will you live?"

Sandra wished her assistant, Eloise, hadn't called in sick with PMS this morning. She felt as if she had stumbled into a play where everyone but her had the script.

"All of your questions will be answered in due time," she announced, a phrase she had acquired from her late husband. She certainly hoped the questions would be answered, and soon.

These past two months, Sandra had heard a few rumblings, but not enough to indicate anything seriously wrong. Her stockbroker had made several inquiries this month, and she'd referred him to Rip Sneed, the lawyer who handled her financial affairs. Then, last week, her banker had called about an overdue loan, and she'd referred him to Rip as well.

When she'd spoken to Rip about the calls, he'd assured her that it was all a misunderstanding concerning a very advantageous major transaction. He said he had run into a short-term cash-flow problem, that was all.

But this didn't sound like a cash-flow problem, unless the press had gotten things wrong. But then again, they often did.

Now, where was her limousine, Sandra wondered as she tried to wedge her way through the crowd of reporters and photographers. Oh, dear, was that a TV crew straight ahead? She couldn't possibly deal with their questions when she was so baffled and confused.

Before her, a uniformed driver appeared like a knight in shining armor, or at least in maroon livery. His violet eyes narrowed against the bright sunshine as he blocked the news crew and ushered Sandra into a white stretch Cadillac.

"Thank you so much. I was overwhelmed," she gasped as he closed the door, shutting out the clamoring hordes. "Is there any grapefruit juice in the bar?"

The chauffeur didn't answer, because he was swinging around the outside of the car. Come to think of it, this didn't look like the limousine Sandra had taken this morning, but she hadn't really been paying attention.

Usually Eloise drove the Rolls-Royce or Sandra piloted the Ferrari, when she was in the mood. That was the wonderful thing about having lots of money. Whatever your mood was, you could indulge it shamelessly.

Sandra hadn't always been rich. Once upon a time she'd been a poor student aspiring to a career in advertising or magazine editing. She had shared a dumpy apartment, a wardrobe and one set of textbooks with her best friend.

Then multimillionaire businessman Malcolm Duval spotted her coming down the library steps. He'd stopped abruptly at the bottom and waited.

She could still remember his delighted smile. He had managed to assess every feminine inch of her with appreciation, but with not a hint of overfamiliarity.

He'd been on campus that day to endow a chair in economics. Instead, after a swift courtship that included candlelight dinners in Monte Carlo and scuba diving off Hawaii, he had endowed Sandra with all his worldly possessions.

What *had* those reporters been talking about? Sandra wondered. Had her lawyer gone bankrupt and killed himself? Surely he knew she would have helped him, if only he'd asked.

Following Malcolm's guidance, first in person and then as scripted in his will, she had entrusted her affairs completely to Rip. It was Malcolm, too, who had hired Eloise, years ago, claiming that Sandra needed someone to screen her phone calls and mail.

It appeared that Eloise might have screened them a little too well. But Sandra still couldn't believe that these two key people in her life had failed her. There must be some reasonable explanation.

The driver pulled out of the parking bay and headed toward the freeway. She took a deep breath. She ought to feel safe now, but her anxiety was building by the second.

Something was wrong. But exactly what? There was

nothing she could do until she got more information, Sandra reflected, and tried to distract herself by studying the chauffeur.

He certainly was handsome. When he turned his head to check for cross traffic, she took in an aristocratic profile that reminded her, in some odd way, of Malcolm's. Maybe it was the haughty tilt of the driver's chin. This most definitely was not the man who'd been driving this morning.

Her mouth suddenly uncomfortably dry, she checked the tiny refrigerator and found it empty. But two hours ago, it had held an assortment of juices and mineral waters!

"Excuse me." She tapped on the glass panel that separated them. The driver pressed a button and it slid open. "I'm afraid this is the wrong car."

"No, ma'am." The driver spoke in a level tone, but his manner was far from deferential. "You are Sandra Duval, aren't you?"

"Certainly!" It offended her that he should be in doubt. Didn't the man read the society pages?

"I was asked to substitute. Your previous driver had a family emergency," the man said, and closed the glass.

It was a plausible excuse. So why did she feel so edgy? Those reporters had upset her. She wished someone would explain what they'd been talking about.

Then she noticed that they were heading southeast on Interstate 5. Her estate in Bel-Air lay to the west.

Malcolm had warned Sandra during their marriage about the risk of being kidnapped. She had been careful ever since to avoid dangerous situations, but those idiotic reporters had made her careless.

She stared out the window at the industrial landscape whizzing by. It would be far too hazardous to jump. Besides, why would someone kidnap her if she had lost all her money?

This last thought skittered around in Sandra's brain, racing frantically here and there until she pounced on it and held it motionless. Then she examined it.

She had lost all her money. Wasn't that what someone had said? How preposterous. A person couldn't lose millions of dollars. Malcolm had left her too well protected for that.

Rip, a round little man whose hair was becoming extinct, had tucked her money safely away in mutual funds and annuities and investments of one sort or another that paid a handsome interest rate. And of course she was a major stockholder in Malcolm's aerospace company.

But it appeared Sneed had committed suicide, or disappeared. Had his "major transaction" blown up? And what about her stockbroker's inquiries and the phone call from the bank last week?

Freeway signs alerted Sandra to the fact that they were passing the Long Beach Freeway. They were definitely heading south from Los Angeles. The driver must have realized his mistake by now, if it *was* a mistake.

She simply had to get home. Besides needing to unravel the confusion about her money, she was expecting more than a hundred birthday guests for dinner at six. It would be a serious breach of etiquette if she wasn't there to greet them.

She tapped on the window again. The man squared his shoulders, an impressive task considering their width, and continued to stare straight ahead.

If only Eloise were here! She always carried Sandra's cellular phone in her oversized purse. But didn't limousines come equipped with phones, too?

There it was, built into the entertainment panel. Perfect! Sandra needed to get information, and she knew exactly where to start.

Cautiously, afraid the driver might try to stop her, she slipped the phone out and tapped in her personal assistant's home number. Eloise had to be there; she was, after all, ill.

"Nickerson residence," said a familiar, nasal voice after two rings.

"Eloise? Thank heavens!" Sandra could feel her blood pressure returning to normal.

"Who's calling, please?" said the voice.

"Eloise, it's me! Sandra!"

"This is Eloise's sister," said the voice. "I'm sorry, she's had to go out of town on a family emergency." Then there was a loud click.

Shocked, Sandra realized that the woman had hung up on her.

A family emergency? Wasn't that what her driver had just claimed had called away the previous chauffeur? Family emergencies seemed to be running rampant today.

But there was a far more sinister interpretation to be put on this matter, and she could not ignore it. That had been Eloise on the phone—not some phantom sister.

There was no emergency. Neither was Eloise in the raging grip of PMS. The truth was that Eloise had somehow got wind of Sandra's crisis, and cruelly abandoned her.

Now that she thought about it, she had only received the banker's call because she had happened to answer the phone herself. Had Eloise been turning away other calls?

Sandra recalled that the doorbell had rung several times yesterday, but Eloise had claimed it was simply the gardeners and pool cleaners.

Maybe her assistant thought it was her job to protect

Sandra from reality. But that wouldn't explain her defection today.

Was it possible Eloise had actually harbored a secret resentment of Sandra's wealth and now was rejoicing in Sandra's troubles? Or perhaps Eloise was so humiliated to learn that she'd tied her wagon to a falling star that she'd chosen to flee rather than stand by her employer in her time of crisis.

Then it hit Sandra that this news must have been circulating late last night or early this morning, while she herself remained ignorant. So that was why the mayor had been avoiding her—the weasel!

She rooted through her purse until she found her phone book, then she dialed Rip Sneed's number. A machine announced that the office was closed.

Next she tried her stockbroker. He had left for the day, his secretary said. He might not be back for a long while.

"Family emergency?" Sandra asked.

"Something like that," said his secretary.

Next she rang her housekeeper at the mansion. Someone picked up the receiver, listened without speaking as Sandra identified herself, then sobbed uncontrollably and hung up.

This was getting worse and worse. Sandra felt like a character in a television program she'd seen once, a woman who went to the supermarket and returned to find that no one recognized her.

Sandra took a mirror from her purse and regarded her image. She looked the same as always: big hat, loosely curled blond hair, blue eyes, straight nose. At least she still recognized herself!

Glancing up, she saw the driver observing her. "Who are you?" Sandra asked.

He shook his head and kept watching her, between surveys of the traffic.

"Where are you taking me?" She was dismayed to hear her voice rise to a near-hysterical level.

The man mouthed something that looked like "to the beach," but she must have misunderstood. You didn't kidnap people and take them to the beach. You snatched them away to some remote spot in a canyon.

That observation somehow failed to reassure her.

She reached for the phone again. There was one person in Los Angeles who could be counted on for complete honesty.

Sandra had to admit she hadn't spent much time recently with her old college roommate. However, that was understandable, now that Belle had a husband and a baby.

Sandra's first act, after inheriting her fortune, had been to buy a staid women's magazine called *Just Us* and transform it into a hip journal for single women. She had hired her old pal, Belle Martens, to edit it, rescuing Belle from a dead-end job in advertising.

Belle had done most of the work of making *Just Us* into a success. Sandra had no head for day-to-day details. She did, however, excel at blowing into the office and devising exciting promotional ideas.

Owning *Just Us* was the one thing that anchored her as she flitted through her busy social schedule. Thanks to the magazine's success, the media occasionally referred to her as a publisher.

She liked that term much better than "socialite." And infinitely better than "pauper."

Sandra simply could not be penniless. A condition she had accepted without question at the age of twenty had become intolerable at thirty-two.

Thirty-two! And with all those guests scheduled to attend her birthday party! Was the caterer there? Had the ice sculpture arrived? Were the alterations complete on her new gown?

Such details might seem trivial, she supposed, but they had to be dealt with. And she'd been *so* looking forward to this party!

Trying hard to get a grip on her growing panic, Sandra dialed the number of the magazine. "Good afternoon, *Just Us*," said a voice on the other end.

"Belle Martens, please." To her immense relief, Sandra was put through at once. "It's Sandra! Belle, you simply must find out what has happened!"

"You're asking me?" Belle said in a ragged voice. "Sandra, there are men here claiming the magazine belongs to a bank. Did you mortgage us?"

"Certainly not!" said Sandra. "Everything was fine until a few minutes ago, and now my money's gone and I've been kidnapped."

"What?" gasped Belle. "Where are you?"

"In a limousine," she said.

"This sounds like a rather luxurious kidnapping," Belle said drily.

"And you should see the driver! He has the absolutely hunkiest shoulders," Sandra admitted. "But he's rather mysterious. Maybe it's a prank, but I can't imagine who would stage something like this."

"Give me your location..." Belle was saying when the phone went dead.

Through the glass, the driver shook his head. Somehow or other, he had cut them off.

In a fit of frustration, Sandra banged on the partition. If only she'd called 911 while she had the chance! She couldn't abide being stuck in this car while her magazine was being shut down and her house overrun by creditors.

And what on earth would happen to her birthday-party guests?

"Let me out!" she yelled.

The driver didn't respond.

She sank back into the seat. They were switching onto the Costa Mesa Freeway, which gave her a faint hope, because Costa Mesa had such a nice shopping mall. It was hard to believe anything terrible could happen in such a lovely town.

Still nursing the faint hope that this would turn out to be a practical joke, Sandra switched on a radio implanted in a panel. After punching several buttons, she located an all-news station.

Following the weather, a traffic report and three commercials, the announcer proclaimed, "Police in Los Angeles today had no further clues to the disappearance of attorney Rip Sneed. Although he was at first believed to have died in the explosion of his yacht in Newport Harbor last night, the Coast Guard now says there were no bodies on board."

So this was what the reporters had meant about a faked suicide. Rip's death, or disappearance, must have triggered the massive press interest and immediate action by the banks.

Sandra supposed it might have been possible for Rip to take out loans against her company and her real estate, loans that had obviously not been repaid. But what had he done with the money?

"Sneed is a suspect in the embezzlement of fifty-three million dollars from Sandra Duval, widow of aerospace magnate Malcolm Duval," the announcer continued. "Mrs. Duval told reporters at the Los Angeles Music Center that she has no comment at this time."

"And I won't ever have one!" Sandra shouted at the

radio. "I refuse to comment about rumors and suspicions! I want facts!"

In the rearview mirror, she caught a pair of glorious violet eyes staring at her with a trace of amusement. Still, glorious violet eyes or not, if there hadn't been a glass partition, Sandra would have taken off her shoe and thrown it at the exasperating man.

When they exited the freeway, she thought again about jumping. On the other hand, she had a strong dislike of physical pain. Besides, the man must be planning to stop soon or he would have stayed on the freeway.

They encountered only green lights for the next few miles, further discouraging any thought of hurling herself from the automobile. After a while, Sandra could see they were descending from coastal bluffs toward the Pacific Ocean.

The man was indeed taking her to the beach. But why? She pressed a button to roll down her window and enjoy the salt air. Nothing happened. Out of curiosity, she tried the door. The latch refused to click.

She was trapped. The driver had not only swept her away from Los Angeles and cut off her telephone, he had locked the doors.

A twinge of panic shot through her. Cocooned amid wealth and luxury for the past twelve years, she hadn't seriously considered that she might be in real danger until now.

Her money had been embezzled by that rat Rip Sneed and Sandra had been abducted.

The fact that her captor possessed the face of a movie star and the physique of a Greek god did nothing to reassure her. She wasn't naive enough to think that real-life villains resembled the scar-faced bad guys in movies.

Still, it seemed a waste that someone so very pleasant to the eye should be so unpleasant inside.

She was still trying to figure out a course of action as they swerved through a series of residential streets and pulled into the driveway of a sprawling, stuccoed house, right alongside the beach.

A few rapid steps would take Sandra into public view. Surely someone would hear her screams. She tensed, preparing herself for the moment of exit.

The partition hummed open. Killing the motor, the driver turned to face her.

There was a continental sophistication about his cheekbones and an ironic twist to his mouth. He studied Sandra as if trying to determine whether she was worth bothering with.

The notion made her bristle. "Well?" she demanded. "Explain yourself!"

"We're going to walk into this house very quietly," the man said. "You won't scream or run away."

"Why not?" she demanded.

"Do you know who this house belongs to?" he asked.

"No," she said. "Should I?"

"It's yours. Or it used to be."

The man might be lying, but Sandra did recall Malcolm mentioning once or twice that they ought to spend a few weeks at the beach house. Somehow they hadn't gotten around to it during their five years of marriage. There had always been a trip to Europe or Fiji, or an invitation to stay with friends in London or Nice or Monte Carlo.

"Mr. Sneed gave me a full accounting of my property after he read the will," she said. "He never mentioned any such house."

"That's because he's been living here," the driver

said. "Would you care to take a look inside? Perhaps he's left some clues to his whereabouts."

"Are you a detective?" she asked.

"Not exactly."

"Why did you lock me in the car?"

"I was afraid you might jump and hurt yourself. I needed to bring you here. You'll see why in a minute." The man came around and opened her door.

Sandra emerged stiffly into the late-afternoon sunshine. The man, she found, was tall, but not excessively so. Despite the width of his shoulders, he didn't have the bulky appearance of a weight lifter, but a solid presence that spoke of self-confident masculinity.

As she brushed past him, she caught a whiff of male spice mixed with motor oil. It gave her a quivery sensation she hadn't experienced in a long time.

Inexplicably, it also carried her back to a moment when she had been twenty years old and had raced down the steps of the library almost into the arms of a very handsome, very rich older man with a smile that would melt cold steel. But this man was neither much older nor rich, Sandra felt sure. And he certainly wasn't smiling.

Twelve years ago, she had let out a slight gasp and gazed upward with startled eyes. This time, she stomped on the man's foot and took off for the beach.

"Hey!" The devil could limp faster than she could run in these ridiculous high heels. At the edge of the sand, the man grabbed tightly on to Sandra's arm.

"That hurt," he said.

"This will hurt even more!" she cried, and raked at him with her fingernails.

He tightened his grip, then suddenly released her. "Go ahead and run. But you'll never get your money back."

She hesitated. She didn't want to believe he held any

power to help her. But there was something about his tone of voice that indicated he was not to be taken lightly.

Besides, he had gone to great lengths to bring her here. Malcolm had always declared that great opportunities required great risks. Sandra felt safe enough out here in public view. She could at least listen to the man.

"Well? What was it you wanted me to see?" Delicately, she removed one shoe and poured out the sand that had sifted in. "What's your name, by the way?"

"Jean-Luc." He stared beyond her, surveying the beach as if expecting intruders.

The name rang a bell, but today there were too many alarms sounding in Sandra's mind for her to place it. "That sounds French."

"My mother was French," said Jean-Luc. "So was my father, if you go back far enough. Now let's get inside."

"You really think this is my house?" Reluctantly, she walked beside him toward the building. It wasn't a large place, but well designed, with clean, modern lines, and the beachfront location must make it worth a million or so.

"I know it beyond any shadow of a doubt." Jean-Luc opened the side door with a key. "Let's hope there's no burglar alarm."

"How did you get a key to my house?" Sandra asked.

"I've had it for years. Don't worry. Everything will be explained in due time," he said, and held the door for her.

That was Malcolm's line. In fact, earlier this afternoon, she had used it herself, she recalled as she entered the house.

Inside, the airy rooms were furnished with wicker and silks. It was just the kind of place her husband would have loved.

There was no clanging or buzzing, thank goodness. "Do you suppose there's a silent alarm?" she asked.

"I doubt it," said Jean-Luc. "The man would be a fool to alert the police when he was living here without your knowledge. Now help me search, will you?"

She peered at the tastefully luxurious surroundings. "For what?"

"An address book. Papers. Letters. Anything Rip Sneed might have left behind," he suggested as he prowled through the rooms. "An answering machine with a message on it would be useful."

She regarded him quizzically. "You brought me here so I could play detective?"

"Not exactly." Jean-Luc turned to regard her. "I'm going to help you get your money back. And you're going to help me, as well. I'm sorry about the kidnapping, but I couldn't think of any other way to whisk you out of that mess. We needed to talk, and we have to take action quickly."

"We?" she said.

"Yes, we," said the man. "We're in this together, you and I."

Sandra shook her head. "I don't even know you. There's no reason on earth why I should trust you."

"Oh, but there is." His chin lifted into the same arrogant tilt that had seemed so familiar earlier. "You know my name. I'm sure you've heard it before."

"Well, possibly," she said. "I mean, I think I have."

"That's it?" He shook his head disapprovingly. "You think you've heard it? I didn't know my father despised me so much he hardly even spoke of me."

"Your father?" she asked with a sinking feeling.

"Malcolm." The young man released a long breath. "Sandra Duvall, I'd like you to meet your stepson—me."

"Your father," she asked with a sinking feeling, "is he rich?" Jac young man shrugged and his breath "Smith. Darcff. I'd use to meet you." How do you

2

————

SEVERAL THINGS suddenly made sense to Sandra. How Jean-Luc got a key to the beach house, for instance. And why he reminded her so much of Malcolm.

It also explained why his name had sounded familiar. After they were married, Malcolm had told Sandra he was estranged from his grown son, and she supposed he must have mentioned the boy's name.

The two had quarrelled years before. Their disagreements had begun when Malcolm wanted his son to major in business so he could take over his father's company, but his son had insisted on studying engineering.

Malcolm had acquiesced, paying for Jean-Luc to attend engineering school, since engineering had some relevance to the aerospace industry. After the young man had graduated, Malcolm made what he had thought was a generous offer. He had proposed to settle a trust fund on his son if Jean-Luc would spend five years working for him.

An argument had developed and tempers had reached a flashpoint. Malcolm had belittled his son's aim of becoming an inventor. Jean-Luc had shouted that he would die before he accepted one penny of his father's money, and he stalked out.

For months afterwards, Malcolm had made sporadic attempts to contact his son. With youthful defiance, Jean-Luc had thrown every overture back in his face. His father, he had claimed, only wanted a son who would become an extension of himself.

After their marriage, Malcolm had revised his will, leaving everything to Sandra. There had been no contact between the two during the five-year marriage, but she had always suspected that, had Malcolm not been cut down abruptly by a heart attack, he might eventually have relented, and reconciled with Jean-Luc.

Now here was Jean-Luc, offering to help Sandra get her fortune back. But why?

"You didn't want your father's money," she reminded him. "What's changed?"

He shifted position. "Look, before we go into any explanations, I'd like to search this place. Rip just cleared out of here recently, so he might have left some clue to his whereabouts. If he did, I need to pass it on to Marcie."

"Who's Marcie?" Sandra couldn't understand why she felt a surge of disappointment at the possibility that Jean-Luc might be married.

"A detective friend of mine. Why don't you check the master bedroom?"

She nodded. If there were any clues, she was in a hurry to find them, too.

While Jean-Luc examined the living room, Sandra located the master bedroom. Through half-open curtains, she could see the Pacific and hear its peaceful rolling hum.

Rip Sneed had cheated her out of this place all these years. That proved what an outright villain he was, she thought in annoyance.

There was nothing under the bed or beneath the mattress. The bureau drawers were empty. A few shelves held a scattering of books and, lying on their sides, there were a couple of movie scripts, probably the bootleg versions available at Hollywood memorabilia outlets. The one on top was *The Godfather*.

In an alcove, Sandra found a small desk but the drawers had been cleaned out. So had the wastebasket. When she moved it, however, Sandra spotted a crumpled wad on the floor.

Retrieving it, she smoothed the paper open. It was a faxed confirmation of a motel reservation in Las Vegas, dated a week ago.

She carried her find to the dining room, where Jean-Luc was rifling the built-in cupboards and paying no attention whatsoever to the splendid view. "What do you make of this?"

His head came up, startled. For a moment, in those violet eyes, Sandra thought she saw a flash of appreciation, the same look she'd seen on Malcolm's face the day they met. But she was probably imagining it.

He examined the sheet of paper. "Good job." He pulled a cell phone from his pocket.

She waited impatiently, listening in on a discussion that was very cryptic. Jean-Luc was asking questions like "Where did he transfer it?" and "Do you have the address?"

After ending the call, he regarded her thoughtfully. "This looks promising," he said. "Marcie's pinpointed a couple of bank accounts with several million dollars in slush money, and she's found a current address for Sneed. I think he'll make a deal rather than go to jail, so we may be able to recover quite a bit."

"I don't understand," Sandra said. "What's he done with my money, and why do you care?"

"I've never liked Rip and I didn't trust him, either." Jean-Luc said, lounging against the wall. "I heard some rumors about him making unusual investments, so about six months ago, I had him checked out."

"I never heard any rumors," she said.

"You don't hang out with computer hackers and techno-freaks, either," he said. "They're the nosiest people on earth. I discovered he was indeed transferring money around in extremely odd ways, but I couldn't be sure he wasn't investing it on your orders."

"Odd ways?" probed Sandra. "What does that mean?"

Her stepson took a deep breath, which rippled through his chest and shoulders in a picturesque way. "He's run some of it through bank accounts in the Cayman Islands, apparently trying to hide the paper trail. What payments I could track down have been made to small entertainment-related firms. Most of them are privately owned, so we can't get hold of their financial records, but I assume he's investing in some kind of movie or video projects."

"He certainly wasn't doing it for me." Sandra felt sick. She also felt furious. "How long has he been at this game?"

"Several years, at least," said Jean-Luc.

"He's been ripping me off practically from the minute Malcolm died!" she said. "That horrible man!"

"What I can't understand," he said, "is why you gave him power of attorney."

"Did I?"

"Apparently so."

She frowned. "I was only twenty-five when Malcolm died. I thought power of attorney was sort of like client confidentiality."

"It's more than that," Jean-Luc said. "You gave him the authority to do anything he liked with your property."

Suddenly Sandra felt very foolish, and she was grateful

to Jean-Luc for not rubbing it in. Despite his unorthodox manner of getting her attention, she was beginning to like him.

Nevertheless, she'd trusted too many people too far. She didn't intend to make the same mistake again now, no matter how appealing her stepson might be.

"What do you get out of this?" she demanded, sitting on a slightly dusty wicker chair. It annoyed her to soil her pink suit, but she was feeling shaky. Besides, she had plenty of clothes to change into.

Used to have, she realized with a pang.

"I need money in a hurry, a lot of it, or I'll lose the opportunity of a lifetime," he said. "Damn, I hate dragging you into this."

"What do you need it for?"

"A friend of mine helped invent a new, lightweight material, heat-resistant and strong," Jean-Luc said. "He and two other men share the rights and they're about to go public. I need to buy the right to use the material for personal helicopters."

"Personal helicopters?" The idea intrigued Sandra. She would love to hop right over traffic. "But wouldn't they be awfully noisy?"

"That's the point—they'd be so lightweight and compact, they wouldn't need powerful, noisy engines." He gazed out at the rolling surf and a sailboat on the horizon. "They'd be so compact, you could keep one in your garage. I've designed the whole thing. I've even built a prototype. I call it the MiniCopter."

"Isn't there anything like it on the market now?" she probed.

"There are small helicopters," he admitted. "But this one leaves them in the dust. It's quieter and more maneuverable, and has enough room inside to seat three adults.''

"So you need money for the right to use their material," Sandra said. "And to go into production, I presume."

"That will come later. Right now, I have to come up with a couple of million dollars by the end of the month," said Jean-Luc. "My friend's partners are eager to auction off the rights. They've agreed to delay a little while on my account, but they're running out of patience."

"I could buy the rights for you," Sandra said. "If I had my money back."

"I'm afraid not. Under the terms of my father's will, you can't invest in my business," Jean-Luc said.

Now that he mentioned it, Sandra did recall a clause forbidding her to give anything to Jean-Luc or else the entire estate would go to charity. It had seemed excessive when Malcolm told her about it, but he said Rip Sneed had suggested it to guard against her softheartedness.

Softheartedness, indeed! No doubt that crook had wanted to make sure he could get his hands on every penny after Malcolm died. He must have been planning his scheme, whatever it was, for a long time.

"I wouldn't have to give you anything," Sandra said. "I could simply pay you for helping me get my money back. Or we could be partners."

Jean-Luc's jaw worked. "The wording is all-inclusive. You can't take any action that will benefit me financially. You can't pay me, give me a loan, invest in my business, subsidize me, transfer funds to my immediate family, even leave me money in your will. Believe me, I've checked this out."

"There's got to be a way around it," she said.

"There is," he said. "We have to get married."

She stared at him. "That's preposterous."

Jean-Luc finger-combed his thick hair. "Under California community-property law, once we commingle our funds, I get half."

"When we divorce," said Sandra.

"Obviously."

"I couldn't possibly do that," she said. "The whole idea is outrageous."

Her stepson flicked a speck of dust from his maroon jacket. "I'll sweeten the deal. After the divorce, you get ten percent of my profits from the helicopters. I doubt you'll earn back as much as you're giving me, but it could be a nice dividend."

"Twenty percent," said Sandra.

"Fifteen."

"Done," she said, then realized what she was committing herself to. "Wait a minute. I can't marry you. That would be incestuous, and possibly illegal."

"I don't see why," said Jean-Luc. "We aren't related by blood. There are probably some cultures in which I would be *forced* to marry you."

"Don't exaggerate."

Marrying her stepson obviously had not been what Malcolm intended. It went against the spirit of his will.

On the other hand, it was Malcolm who had entrusted their entire estate to Rip. Without Jean-Luc, Sandra was left with nothing, and that hadn't been her late husband's intention, either.

"There has to be another way to resolve this mess," she said. "May I borrow your phone?"

He shrugged and handed it over.

From Information, she got the name of a top Hollywood attorney, Horace Alonzo, who had handled several famous civil suits. To Sandra's relief, Alonzo took her call right away.

"Of course, I'll be happy to represent you," he said when she explained why she was calling.

"Do you think we can get my money back?"

"I have as good an investigative team as you'll find anywhere," Alonzo said. "Then we'll bring suit for recovery."

"I don't have any money to pay you," she said. "Not at the moment."

"That's all right," said Alonzo. "I'll work on contingency. Thirty percent."

"Thirty percent?" Sandra repeated, dumbfounded. "Thirty percent of fifty-three million dollars?"

"Or whatever we recover," he said pleasantly.

"I'll get back to you," she said, and clicked off. "Thirty percent! That's outrageous! I can't possibly work with that man! He's a highway robber."

"Well?" asked Jean-Luc. "You're certainly taking your time responding to my proposal. I'm sorry I forgot the flowers. Would you like to see me get down on one knee?"

She managed a smile, her first in hours. Marrying Jean-Luc was beginning to sound less and less outrageous. Of course, he expected fifty percent, even more than Alonzo, but he was Malcolm's son and he was offering her a share in his business. "How long do you think it will take Marcie to recover the slush fund?"

"Maybe as little as twenty-four hours, if she's as close as she thinks," he said.

A few million dollars might be enough to stave off Sandra's creditors until she and Jean-Luc could untangle the rest of the maze. Relief flooded through her. In another day, her life could return to normal! Well, semi-normal.

The fact that she would be marrying a man who was her own stepson and a total stranger was a bit touchy. But it wouldn't be a real marriage, Sandra assured herself. It was merely a legal convenience to get around the will.

They would write their names on a piece of paper, an ordinary contract. A few days or weeks later, when the time was right, they would sign some more papers and poof! be divorced.

"Well?" said Jean-Luc. "Will you marry me a little?"

"I think so," she said. "Why not?"

"Thank goodness." He checked his watch. "We've just got time to get to the county clerk's office before it closes."

"Isn't there a waiting period?" she asked. "Don't we need blood tests?"

"Not these days." He tucked the fax into his uniform pocket. "And I've already got the limousine."

HIS FATHER KNEW how to pick them, all right, Jean-Luc reflected, taking a sidelong glance at Sandra as he drove.

In her day, his mother had been a celebrated beauty. Sandra didn't compare, of course, but at close range she was prettier than he'd expected.

His impression of his stepmother from glimpsing her on television had been of a dizzy blonde with blue sky shining through the back of her head. In person, she was loopy, all right, but with a maddening logic and a certain charm.

The woman radiated contradictions. How could she be so foolish one minute and so intelligent the next?

What the TV cameras had also failed to capture was

her spontaneous sexuality. It came across as artless, almost naive. Yet the woman had to realize that her skin glowed like velvet and her body moved with the slow sensuality of a lazing cat.

But he didn't intend to let her affect him. Sandra might have her appealing qualities, but any woman clever enough to have snared Malcolm was no innocent. For all he knew, she had approached his father with the same calculated determination that Jean-Luc's ex-wife, Nora, had used when she enticed him to the altar.

He didn't like the way Sandra's perfume kept distracting him from the tasks ahead. He didn't like wondering how it would feel to touch her soft skin, or to pull her against him, or to spend the night in her bed.

Jean-Luc had no intention of doing any of those things. He had too many commitments and responsibilities to let himself get sidetracked.

He thrust her out of his mind and focused on his driving.

SANDRA EXPERIENCED a moment of anxiety as they approached the courthouse in Santa Ana. A marriage contract wasn't *exactly* like an ordinary contract. How could she take such a risk?

She had no proof that this was really Jean-Luc, she reflected as they parked behind the building. What if she found herself married to an opportunistic fraud?

But she had only to look at him to see the resemblance to Malcolm. It was there in his confident manner, his aquiline nose, and the twist of his lips when annoyed. It would be there in his driver's license, too, when he presented his ID to the clerk.

It did seem odd to be getting married. If anyone had asked Sandra this morning what was on the agenda, she would have listed the charity breakfast, the music-center luncheon and, of course, her birthday party. No kidnappings, no disappearing fortunes, and definitely no weddings.

The car stopped. With a jaunty step, Jean-Luc came around and held the door open.

As she slipped out, Sandra wondered what he thought of her. He didn't treat her like a stepmother, but he didn't treat her like a fiancée, either.

Not that she wanted him to. Muscular builds and intense, burning expressions weren't her cup of tea. She preferred a man to be adoring and pliant.

"How can you be sure Sneed hasn't lost the money?" she asked as Jean-Luc escorted her into the building. "If he did invest in films, they may have been bombs."

"Or hits," he pointed out. "Besides, he's not dealing with any major film studios. These are specialized companies that find locations, cast roles, edit film and so forth. I think he may have put together a speculative investment in the video business, possibly a line of CD-ROMs."

"That doesn't sound so bad," said Sandra.

"Definitely not," agreed the man she was about to marry. "In today's market, it could be very lucrative. I suspect he intended to repay all those loans and mortgages without your knowledge, but ran into some setbacks."

Where money was concerned, it didn't take Sandra long to sort out the implications. "You mean he might actually increase the investment? When he gets past these setbacks, that is?"

"Possibly." Gritting his teeth, Jean-Luc added, "If he returns the full amount he stole, we can offer to let him keep his profit. I'd hate to see him come out ahead, but it might be in our best interest to avoid lengthy litigation.''

At least her future husband was reasonable, she reflected. ''But first we conduct a complete audit of my assets *and* his, to make sure he's not hiding anything.''

''Absolutely.''

They waited at the end of a short line. Ahead of them, men and women stood with arms wrapped around each other. One couple was kissing. No one else, as far as she could tell, was discussing audits or assets.

It gave Sandra the sense that she'd gotten in the wrong line. It also made her miss Malcolm. Their relationship hadn't been very passionate, but it had been tender.

She found herself wishing that, just for show, Jean-Luc would slip an arm around her waist. Maybe he could nuzzle her hair, for appearance's sake. The thought sent a quiver through her.

A quick glance showed him staring straight ahead. There was no cuddling on his mind, as far as she could see.

They finally reached a clerk, who gave them some papers to fill out. Under the section for previous marriages, Sandra jotted the information.

Then she noticed that Jean-Luc was writing in that section, too. ''You were married before?''

He finished and looked up. ''We've been divorced three years. My wife expected me to inherit a fortune. After it became clear I never would, she started looking for someone with better prospects. Eventually, she found him.''

No wonder the man seemed bitter, Sandra thought. His father had disinherited him and his wife had cast him off.

Yet in the proud carriage of Jean-Luc's shoulders, she saw a man whom the world could never beat down. He would go his own way at any cost, and without deference to anyone. Which, she reflected, was how he'd become estranged from his father in the first place.

He signed them up for a confidential marriage. That meant, the clerk explained, that no one but the two of them could obtain copies of the marriage certificate.

Sandra couldn't believe her luck. They could marry with utter discretion, for only $71.25.

Jean-Luc had come equipped with cash. He had also brought a gold wedding ring, which was probably either a good fake or left over from his marriage. She didn't care to ask which.

He had been correct: no blood tests were required. After obtaining the license, they went down the hall to wait for a marriage commissioner who, for an additional thirty-one dollars, would perform the ceremony.

Sandra wondered how the county had come up with odd amounts like $71.25 and thirty-one dollars. She supposed some employee with nothing better to do had written whimsical amounts on slips of paper, dropped them into a hat and asked passersby to pick one. It seemed democratic, at least.

She said her vows and signed her name, glad that she'd worn her pink suit and a hat trimmed with roses. The outfit did have a more or less bridal air.

Her wedding to Malcolm had been less hasty but equally discreet. They had eloped to Palm Springs, where they were married by a judge with a thick mustache. She'd worn a white sundress and a Little Bo Peep hat.

Jean-Luc slipped the ring onto her finger. It was slightly loose, but Sandra supposed she could wrap string around it, the way she'd done years ago with a boyfriend's class ring.

When her husband made no move to kiss her, the marriage commissioner's eyebrow quirked upward. Determined to do this properly, Sandra stood on tiptoe and brushed her lips across Jean-Luc's cheek.

His skin had an edge of roughness, and once again she caught the faint scent of motor oil. His breath quickened, and she felt his hand caress her shoulder.

She wondered what it would be like to make love to Jean-Luc in his limousine, then drew back quickly. They were not going to consummate this marriage. Even if they did, she certainly wouldn't do it in a car.

She had been a virgin when she married Malcolm, and had remained chaste since his death. Intercourse with her husband had been pleasant, but she saw no point in engaging in that sweaty, overrated activity with anyone else.

Still, she wished Jean-Luc had kissed her back. His mouth had a delicious curve to it that she wanted to explore.

If he felt the same way, however, Jean-Luc didn't show it as he guided her back to the limo. With her ensconced in the front passenger seat, they headed west toward Los Angeles.

Sandra's thoughts simply wouldn't behave themselves. As soon as they settled onto the freeway, she began wondering what her new husband would look like without that starchy uniform. It didn't fit him well, anyway. It strained at the shoulders, and cut him at the waist.

It also did nothing to disguise Jean-Luc's animal grace, as if his ancestors had left the wild only a few generations ago. That broad chest simply begged to have its buttons ripped away. Not that Sandra had ever ripped anyone's buttons, but it seemed a provocative idea, as long as she didn't have to sew them on again.

My husband. She had never expected to say those

words again, even for twenty-four hours. She had imagined that she could never marry because there was no one she could trust. They all wanted her money.

So what had she done? Married a man who wanted her money, that's what.

An hour later, they emerged from the maze of freeways in an area she didn't recognize. "Where are we?"

"Manhattan Beach," said Jean-Luc. "Marcie will contact us at a motel here as soon as she reaches Rip."

"Marcie knew we were getting married?" Sandra asked in dismay.

"Sure."

"When? When did she know?"

"Last night. What's the difference?" He steered the limo along streets that narrowed as they neared the ocean.

"I just wondered how many people on this earth knew I was getting married before I did," she said.

"Only two." Jean-Luc swung the elongated car into the parking lot of a motel.

"Well, that's a relief," said Sandra.

He angled the limo until it slid into two spaces, front to back. "Be careful how you open the door. I have to take the car back tomorrow."

"Take it back?" she asked. "You rented it?"

"Borrowed," he said. "I own a garage. The limo had to be repaired, and the owner isn't picking it up until tomorrow afternoon."

"You mean you took it without permission?" she asked. "That's stealing!"

"It needed a test drive," he said, and helped her out.

In the office, they registered as Mr. and Mrs. Duval. It struck Sandra that one advantage to marrying her stepson was that she didn't have to change her name.

She had no bags, but Jean-Luc fetched his suitcase

from the trunk. He led the way into Room 103, which was labeled the Honeymoon Suite for no discernible reason.

The room came equipped with a bed that might have been large enough for two people if one of them was a chimpanzee. The chest of drawers listed to the side, and the only decoration was a plastic-encased copy of *TV Guide* attached to the wall by a looped telephone cord.

"It's lovely," Sandra said drily.

Jean-Luc flipped open the suitcase and took out a pair of chenille pajamas that might have been cut from an old bedspread. "Marcie thought you could use something like this."

Repressing the temptation to say "for what?" she hung the pajamas in the closet. "It's kind of her to take such an interest in my welfare." She couldn't help adding, "Is Marcie going to be the future Mrs. Duval? After our unfortunate breakup?"

"Marcie?" His face reflected astonishment. "Good lord, no. She's my cousin."

"On your late mother's side," said Sandra.

"Yes," he agreed, removing his clothes from the suitcase. "Why?"

"Otherwise I might have met her," she pointed out.

Tossing several garments over his arm, Jean-Luc stepped into the bathroom but left the door ajar. From the sound of garments being stripped away, she realized he was removing his uniform.

Irreverently, she wondered what kind of underpants he wore. Probably the tight-fitting kind, not baggy like Malcolm's. The rest of his body would be tight-fitting, too. She didn't care to speculate about whom it might fit tightly into.

The man emerged wearing a T-shirt and jeans. The

clothes might as well have been spray-painted on his body, the way they revealed every taut muscle. She could picture him standing in his garage, a sweaty mechanic, tossing aside his wrench and leading a lady customer into the back room....

Sandra slapped her own cheek.

"Are you all right?" Her husband regarded her quizzically.

"I was getting hysterical," she said.

"It's probably hunger." He started for the door. "There's a Chinese restaurant down the block. Care to get some takeout?"

Sandra's feet ached, but she did want to go out. "Couldn't we eat there?"

"We can't risk being spotted. You never know where the media will show up." Jean-Luc paused in the doorway. "If Rip Sneed sees us together on the news, he'll figure out that we've joined forces to catch him. Then we can kiss our chances goodbye."

They couldn't take that risk. Nothing must interfere with recovering her money. "You go." She kicked off her shoes. "I'll wait here."

"You sure?" At her nod, Jean-Luc departed, leaving Sandra to wonder what she was doing in this tacky hotel room, married to a stranger, and whether she had completely lost her mind.

3

As soon as she was alone, Sandra put in a call to Belle at home.

"What happened to the magazine?" she asked. "They didn't close it down, did they?"

"Certainly not!" Belle returned. "The bank considers us a valuable asset. As a matter of fact, I'm planning to ask for a raise."

"Let me know what they think you're worth," said Sandra. "When I get my money back, I'll match it."

"Is this an actual possibility? Recovering the money, I mean?" Belle asked. "Where are you, by the way? Everybody's asking."

She sketched in the day's events.

"Unbelievable," said Belle when Sandra was finished. "Nobody but you would do such a crazy thing. And knowing you, you'll come out of it smelling like a rose."

A baby started crying in the background.

"Susan's hungry?" Sandra asked. "Or does she need her diaper cleaned?"

"Changed," Belle corrected. "I wish Darryl would get home. I try to encourage paternal participation in diaper changing as much as possible. Listen, I can't help you much with the money hunt, but I'll do my best to keep the magazine together. If they try to sell it, I'll stall."

"How?" she asked.

"I'll threaten to quit."

"You'd do that?" Sandra was impressed.

"I said threaten," Belle replied. "I didn't say I'd actually leave."

"That's good enough," she said. "Please don't tell anyone what's happened or where I am."

"I wouldn't dream of it."

"You don't know how much I appreciate this." As she said goodbye, she heard another wail from the background. Sandra was glad that at least she didn't have to deal with a baby, on top of all her other problems.

Some people weren't cut out to have kids, and she was one of them. She had once summed up the subject for Belle by saying, "I know so little about children, I keep mistaking them for mice. When one enters the room, I scream."

If only she could also find it in her heart to be so blithe about losing her fortune, marrying a man who didn't love her and having her birthday party turn into the social debacle of the century.

JEAN-LUC HALF EXPECTED to find his new wife gone when he returned, but she was lying on the bed watching television. She wore only the chenille pajama top.

Like Marcie's other clothes, it lacked anything approaching style, but Sandra had left the top two buttons undone, revealing a delicious hint of cleavage. From beneath the top stretched long, slender legs, tantalizingly bare.

As Jean-Luc angled into the room, balancing several sacks of Chinese food, his gaze lingered on the open neck of the pajamas and the upper swell of two perfectly rounded breasts. With her almost translucent skin and mass of blond curls, Sandra might as well have been wearing a sign that said, "Make love to me."

How could she look so appealing in pajamas that made his cousin Marcie resemble a twelve-year-old boy?

"What are you watching?" he asked.

The saddest blue eyes he had ever seen turned toward him. "I'm waiting for my birthday party," she said.

Jean-Luc couldn't suppress a twinge of pity. He didn't want to like this woman, but he had to admit she'd been a good sport about sharing her once-and-future fortune with him. And she hadn't personally done anything to deserve this turn of events.

It wasn't Sandra's fault that Jean-Luc's dreams had clashed with his father's plans. It wasn't her fault that the two of them had possessed quick tempers and stubborn natures. Especially Jean-Luc.

Tossing aside his share of a fortune had seemed like a noble declaration of independence at the age of twenty-one. Thirteen years later, he could see it had been mere stubbornness, and not a little stupidity. It had certainly not occurred to him that his father might die suddenly, without a chance at reconciliation.

The past couldn't be changed, but the future could. He was doing his best to correct old mistakes, Jean-Luc told himself.

He handed Sandra a white paper carton and settled on the other side of the bed. He tried not to notice what a forlorn figure she made, sitting there digging around with wooden sticks while tears glimmered in her eyes.

For twelve years, since his father's marriage, Sandra had remained a remote figure whom Jean-Luc regarded with vague dislike. He had supposed she was money-hungry like his ex-wife Nora.

If she was, at least Sandra's motives must have been obvious to a man as experienced as Malcolm, so she hadn't taken advantage of her husband. On the other hand, Jean-Luc had been naive enough to think he was loved for himself, not merely because he was the son of a rich man.

Well, he'd been wrong about Nora. He'd been wrong about Sandra, too, in a different way.

When he planned today's abduction, he had expected to encounter a cold, calculating female who held no attraction for him whatsoever. He hadn't expected this assault on his senses. Even above the Chinese food, he caught whiffs of the exotic perfume that had stimulated him in the car.

He hadn't anticipated the sweetness of her woebegone expression, either. Nor the way a strand of hair kept creeping onto her forehead, forcing her to brush it away repeatedly, like a distracted child.

The lady aroused his protective instincts. Jean-Luc couldn't understand why. Usually he preferred self-sufficient women, not waifs. Besides, the only thing Sandra needed protecting from was her own bad judgment about her lawyer, he told himself irritably.

On TV, her image came into view. There was the Music Center, with Sandra standing out in front wearing that ridiculous hat and announcing blithely, "All of your questions will be answered in due time."

The phrase struck Jean-Luc. He hadn't recognized until now that he, like her, must have learned it from his father. He wondered what other influences they shared.

"I could be mistaken for a grand duchess in that hat," observed the woman beside him as she stared at the screen. It was impossible to tell from her tone whether she considered that a good thing, or not.

The picture switched to two news anchors sitting at a newsroom desk. "In a moment, we'll show you the scene at this hour at Sandra Duval's Bel-Air mansion," said the male anchor.

"Guests continue to arrive, many apparently unaware that their hostess no longer owns the house," added the female anchor.

The picture switched to a tree-lined circular driveway where uniformed valets were speaking with the drivers of a long line of Rolls-Royces, stretch limousines and Porsches. One by one, the cars departed without discharging their passengers.

Jean-Luc felt no particular nostalgia for the vast house visible in the background. His parents had bought it when he was a teenager, and it had always struck him as luxurious but cold, more like a five-star hotel than a home.

Its vast rooms were filled with untouchable vases and sculptures. He had only been allowed to hold a few, small parties at the pool house. That pool house was bigger than the apartment where he had lived for the past eight years.

"There's my favorite director. I never thought he'd come!" said Sandra as a sports car zoomed out of camera range. "And to be turned away like that—how humiliating!"

"It's not your fault," he said.

"Yes, it is." She grimaced. "I shouldn't have trusted Rip Sneed. If I'd screwed up my investments myself, at least I would have done it honestly."

This flash of responsibility impressed him. In Jean-Luc's experience, most people sought to blame their problems on someone else.

But that didn't change the fact that she *had* managed to lose more than fifty million dollars through sheer carelessness. And, watching the parade of famous and celebrated faces on the screen, he experienced a flash of resentment.

For the past seven years, Sandra had been throwing sumptuous parties and buying designer clothes with the inheritance that should have gone to him. Even though he knew it was his own fault, it cut him to see the lights glimmering in the trees and the hired valets, and to think of the thousands of dollars worth of food and decorations that must have been ordered.

If he had had that money, he wouldn't be wasting his days running a garage. He could have put some of his inventions into production and made a name for himself that would have rivaled that of his father.

Investment capital was tight these days, not like half a century ago when his father started out in the aerospace industry. Even a loan guarantee would have helped, but Malcolm had denied him everything.

Well, if Sandra was willing to take responsibility for her mistakes, so was Jean-Luc. He'd blown his chances at his father's fortune once, but he wouldn't do it again. And he would use Malcolm's money as he knew his father would have wished, to help a new generation of Duvals.

The twins had been born a year after their grandfather's death. The pregnancy had been an accident, but one that delighted Jean-Luc.

Nora hadn't felt the same way. She'd barely stuck around until the kids were in preschool, and even before that she'd been gone most evenings, singing at a nightclub. They could have scraped by without the money, but she enjoyed getting out, so Jean-Luc tried to be supportive.

One night she'd come home and announced she'd met someone new. A rich someone, as it had turned out. Nora had signed over full custody and gotten a divorce so fast she left half her clothes behind.

The twins were a handful, each with separate needs and demands, but just the thought of them warmed Jean-Luc. He loved how they flung their arms around him every evening, and the way they expressed their funny six-year-old views of the world. This past year had been a humbling and thrilling experience as they went through first grade and became in subtle ways more independent.

Thank goodness he had a downstairs neighbor who was willing to babysit in exchange for auto repairs. She had a real fondness for the children, and a very old car.

A soft noise drew his attention to the woman beside him. With the back of her hand, Sandra brushed away the tears streaming down her cheeks. Catching his glance, she wiped her face quickly on one sleeve.

Maybe he should have told her about the twins, Jean-Luc mused. But he couldn't see what difference it would make. He and Sandra would be parting ways quickly, maybe as soon as tomorrow.

Since he'd promised her a share of his company, they would stay in contact. But she would have no part in his daily life, and she might never meet the kids.

On TV, the female anchor said, "The big mystery tonight is, what has happened to Sandra Duval? No one has seen her since she stepped into a limousine at the music center."

"Belle Martens, editor of *Just Us* magazine, was the last person to hear from Mrs. Duval," offered the male anchor. "She told us earlier that she received a phone call in which Mrs. Duval claimed she was being kidnapped, but didn't seem very concerned about it."

"Authorities believe this is a ruse and that the socialite-publisher has gone into hiding," added his colleague.

"Anyone knowing of Mrs. Duval's whereabouts is asked to notify her personal assistant, Eloise Nickerson, at 310-555-5779."

"Eloise? That traitor?" yelled Sandra. "Never! I will never call that Quisling, that Benedict Arnold, that yellow-bellied turncoat!"

"Remind me not to get on your bad side," said Jean-Luc, removing her carton before she could dribble the remains of the Mongolian chicken on the bed.

"I haven't got a bad side," she replied calmly. "All the photographers say so. But then, I pay them rather well." She gave him a teasing smile that almost immediately dissolved into tears.

Setting aside his own empty carton, Jean-Luc gathered her to him. The tousled head came down against his chest and she snuggled close, curling as if to make herself as small as possible.

With one arm, he encircled her shoulders. With the other hand, he lifted the remote control and switched channels until he found a cable program about innovations in technology.

The segment on miniature robots capable of traveling through the bloodstream failed to distract him from the warmth of Sandra's body. He could feel her breasts pressing into his side, and her breath whispering along his chest.

She had thrown one knee over his thigh, and heat radiated from her core onto his hip. Jean-Luc wondered what it would be like to roll her over and explore her curves at his leisure.

He could feel himself grow hard with desire. Damn it, he'd stayed clear of involvements since Nora left, and the last person on earth he wanted to have an affair with was his wife. His sort-of-wife.

After a few minutes, her regular breathing told him she had fallen asleep. He considered shifting her away from him, but was afraid he'd wake her.

Grimly, Jean-Luc settled down to a long, uneasy night with the remote control on one side and temptation on the other.

SANDRA AWAKENED to see sunlight streaming through cheap, stained curtains. For a moment, she thought she was back in her apartment with Belle and that she must be late for class.

Then she heard a low, insistent knock at the door and remembered where she was. Beside her, a rumpled Jean-Luc swung to his feet, and she saw that he was still dressed.

They had slept in the same bed all night. Sandra couldn't imagine how she had allowed that. At the same time, she wished he would come back because the bed felt cold without him.

He pried open the door and a young woman slipped through. Of medium height, she was chunky, with straight black hair and violet eyes like Jean-Luc's. His cousin, obviously.

The newcomer might have been attractive had she worn makeup and something other than a loose-fitting flannel shirt and jeans above dirty jogging shoes. That lank hair could use a bit of work, too.

"Well?" Jean-Luc demanded, closing the door behind their visitor.

"He's gone." Marcie shot a curious gaze at Sandra. "But I've got some more leads."

"What do you mean, gone?" he demanded. "I thought we had him. And the money. Weren't there a couple of bank accounts...?"

"Drained," admitted his cousin. "He's one step ahead of us. This new Las Vegas connection is troubling."

"You think he's gambling?" Jean-Luc began pacing. He was obviously a man in need of morning coffee, and this was not the sort of hostelry that provided it.

"I certainly hope not. I just don't know what he's up to." Marcie twirled a strand of hair around her finger. "I can't believe she went along with this. You two actually got married?"

"Embezzlement makes for strange bedfellows," said Sandra. "You must be Marcie."

The two women shook hands. Marcie's grip was firm and abrupt.

"I saw you on the news last night," she said.

"Why?" demanded Jean-Luc. "You were supposed to be working."

"I *was* working," said his cousin. "I was asking questions in a bar and they had the TV on. Wow. Sandra Duval in person. I can't believe it."

"Thanks for the pajamas," she said.

"They look better on you than on me," Marcie admitted.

"Can the small talk, will you?" muttered Jean-Luc. "You told me you could get your hands on the man in twenty-four hours."

Marcie shrugged. "I was wrong. So? Did I hold it over your head when you forgot to reconnect my radiator hose and it went dry halfway to Palm Springs?"

"I get your point," he said. "When do you think you'll find him?"

"I'm heading to Vegas," she said. "I've got a couple of leads on where the money might have gone. Did you tell Sandra he keeps renting empty stores? We can't figure out why."

"Some kind of scam?" she suggested. "Selling counterfeit merchandise?"

"Maybe, except we can't find that he's bought any stock to sell," Marcie said. "You guys want to come with me? Many hands make light work."

"And too many cooks spoil the broth," noted Jean-Luc. "I've got work to do at the garage. Somebody has to make a living around here."

"Sandra?" asked Marcie.

She sneaked a glance at her husband. He was glowering. Obviously, he didn't want her to go, probably because she might be recognized. "Some other time."

"I'll call you when I get there." The dark-haired woman gave them both an apologetic smile. "We'll nab this sucker sooner or later."

"Sooner, please God," said Jean-Luc.

When his cousin had gone, he disappeared into the bathroom. Sandra wondered whether the bank had canceled her credit cards. She needed some beach clothes and a swimsuit, not to mention cosmetics, sunglasses and a hat.

When Jean-Luc emerged a few minutes later, he pulled down the suitcase and began throwing in his toiletry items. "Well?" he said. "You'd better get ready."

She stifled a yawn. "For what?"

"As I mentioned, I have to work at the garage," explained her husband. "Since apparently we're stuck with each other for a while, you can make yourself useful."

"Useful?" Sandra's eyes widened at the image of herself in a blue coverall, wallowing in grease. "I don't know a wrench from a—a—a whatchamacallit."

"I don't expect you to fix cars!" he chuckled. "Is that what you thought?"

She didn't find it funny. "What do you need, a recep-

tionist? I could handle that, I guess.'' She liked meeting
the public and, from her work at the magazine, she'd kept
up with her computer skills.

''I had something a bit more old-fashioned in mind.''
From the closet, Jean-Luc tossed her the pink suit. It was
wrinkled but passable, she supposed. Her hat was another
matter. Despite the water in tiny vials, the roses drooped.

''Old-fashioned?'' If he expected Sandra to cook, the
man was in for a rude shock.

His next words sent a chill down her spine. ''I've pre-
vailed on my neighbor long enough. You'll have to watch
the kids.''

''Whose kids?''

''Mine,'' replied her new husband. ''Six-year-old
twins, a boy and a girl. Think you can manage that?''

''No,'' she said. ''Don't you have day care?''

''It's expensive. Besides, the kids prefer being at
home.'' He regarded her with amusement. ''Come on,
it's not that difficult.''

''Not to you, maybe,'' Sandra said. ''Are they still in
diapers? I couldn't possibly change one. And what if they
jump out the window?''

''You'll figure it out,'' said Jean-Luc pitilessly. ''After
all, you're their stepmother.''

She shivered. ''*Stepmother.* It sounds so—so ma-
tronly!''

He grinned at her so hard she thought her pajamas
might burst into flames. ''Would you rather they called
you their grandmother? Because you're that, too.''

A frisson of horror ran through Sandra. She had just
turned thirty-two. She hadn't developed so much as a
gray hair yet, and if she did, her coiffeur would kill it
like a deadly virus.

If word got out that she was a grandmother, the gossip

would never cease. People would say she had faked her birth date, had her face and body sculpted and lied to her friends.

Senior citizens were more active and vital than ever these days. But she wasn't ready to be one yet, not by a long shot.

"Stepmother would be fine," said Sandra.

would reverberate. People would squint and stare...
Carrie

4

AT THE TOP of a flight of nubbly cement steps, Sandra
stood on a narrow walkway and peered into the dark
lodgings that Jean-Luc called home.

She tried hard to see the possibilities. The apartment
was not a total loss. For example, it had walls.

There was also, she recognized, a couch, or at least a
worn, lumpy piece of furniture masquerading as one. The
shag carpet gave the impression of overgrown grass, right
down to the color.

She didn't see any toys. A tiny flame of hope sprang
up in Sandra's heart. Maybe Jean-Luc had been joking
about the children.

Cautiously, she stepped inside. The air smelled fresh,
at least. There was none of the heavy dustiness that
would testify to inadequate cleaning.

Score one for the Duval Family, Jr.

Swiveling, Sandra let her gaze sweep across the television set and a small bookcase. At the front window,
heavy curtains of a muddy hue blocked all but a sliver
of the view, which was quite excellent, really. One could
see the entire parking lot from here.

Her survey ended at the doorway, where Jean-Luc's
sculpted frame blocked all hope of escape. "Welcome
home," he said.

"It's..." Sandra's hands fluttered as she searched for
the right word. "...nostalgic."

"Excuse me?"

Did the man have to pin her down to precise meanings? She felt like a butterfly being nailed to a page. "It reminds me of a place where I used to live. When I was younger."

He studied her with a violet gaze that seemed to search into her soul and find it wanting. "No wonder you were so eager to marry my father."

"We had fun there, Belle and I," she said. "Besides, I married Malcolm for love. Everybody knows that."

"Do they?"

"You really ought to see a therapist about your sour view of life," she said, and was about to point out that it couldn't be healthy for the children, when she remembered that it might be best not to mention the little darlings. Perhaps, if she didn't, Jean-Luc would forget about them. "Shall we take the grand tour?"

"By all means." With a hint of a smile, he offered her his arm. Sandra took it with a tiny curtsy that set the wilted roses nodding atop her hat.

They turned to the right, where they discovered the kitchen. It had worn linoleum, faded print curtains, a square wooden table and an assortment of aging appliances.

There was also, she noticed with relief, the most important appliance of all: a telephone. Food was only a dial tone away.

Even more delightfully, nothing crunched or rolled underfoot. If children had been here, they had done a noble job of cleaning up.

Perhaps—since she couldn't entirely bring herself to believe that Jean-Luc had invented their existence—what he had were a pair of those precocious youngsters whom one witnessed on television. Sandra knew what she would do with them. She would find agents for the little charmers, and arrange movie contracts, and send them off to the studio each morning with a chaperone.

There was a solution for everything, if one only knew where to look.

Retreating from the kitchen presented a problem. On entering, she and Jean-Luc had both managed to fit through the door without awkwardness, but when they tried to exit, they kept colliding. Intertwining. Trying to let the other go first, and then botching it.

If only he weren't so much larger than she was, with shoulders and a chest that managed to be in several places at the same time. Sandra found herself wondering, after his arm grazed her breasts just as his thigh brushed her hip, whether he could manipulate the other parts of his anatomy with similar finesse.

It was not a question she cared to answer through personal experimentation, she decided, and stopped dead. With a bow, Jean-Luc gestured her out.

She strolled through the living room and entered a tiny corridor in which the shadows lay deep, even in midmorning. Opening from it were three portals: one directly ahead and one on each side. A bathroom and two bedrooms, she guessed, and turned toward the door on her right.

As she started to turn the knob, Jean-Luc said from behind her, "You don't really want to go in there."

"Wild animals?" she guessed. Was it possible he kept his children locked inside, caged like beasts who would leap upon her and lick her to death if freed?

"Toys," he said. "The rule around here is, I don't care what their room looks like as long as the rest of the house is clear. They just kind of throw stuff in, and if it toppled on you, well, I'm not sure what the paramedic response time is around here.''

Sandra didn't know, either. Actually, she wasn't familiar with this area of Southern California. They'd driven inland a considerable distance, departing civilization for the uncharted regions that lay between Orange County and Palm Springs.

She felt much as Columbus must have, or Marco Polo, or *The Borrowers Afloat*. It was best not to invite trouble in such an alien landscape.

The bathroom was small, more of a powder room really. She appreciated the way the rubber decals in the tub coordinated with the splotchy flowers on the shower curtain.

Suction-cupped to the tile wall was a plastic container packed with tiny boats, yellow ducks, and some fat, rubbery books meant to be read while bathing. Their protagonist appeared to be someone named Spot.

At last they came to the master bedroom. It had a newer carpet, short-haired and russet, installed after the last heavy rain, Jean-Luc mentioned.

Sandra contemplated the full-length mirror fronting a narrow closet, the defiantly squatty bureau and the bed. One bed, arguably a double, if neither person breathed.

''We shall have to make sleeping arrangements,'' she said. ''Does the sofa open?''

''No, but you can have it if you like.'' Jean-Luc shrugged. ''It's too short for me.''

Perhaps, Sandra thought, she could depart before tonight. But it seemed unlikely Marcie could rustle up any cash that quickly.

A million or so would do nicely. It seemed so little to ask.

The other alternatives held less appeal. Even if she

wished to run up her credit-card balance, Sandra had no desire to stay in some cheesy motel by herself. If she was truly desperate, she knew Belle would put her up, but it wouldn't take long for the press to find her there.

She might as well make the best of things. "Whatever," she said.

"I've got to get to work." Jean-Luc ran one hand through his crisp brown hair. Sandra could have sworn she saw fear flash through his eyes, and then he said, "It's time to relieve my neighbor of the children. Do your best with them, will you?"

"I always do my best," she said, and hoped he didn't realize they would all have been safer taking a nice cruise on board the Titanic.

JEAN-LUC HAD EXPECTED her to walk through the apartment with her nose in the air. Instead, she'd given no hint that she was inspecting anything less than a castle.

Perhaps, he admitted grudgingly, he hadn't been entirely fair to his father. Malcolm was nobody's fool. He wouldn't have married a blatant gold digger, or a snob.

Still, abandoning the children to her care seemed a bit risky. The woman was so impulsive, she might accidentally set the place on fire.

Or, more likely, set *him* on fire, Jean-Luc reflected. His skin still tingled at the memory of how she'd curled against him last night.

Despite her drooping hat and crinkled suit, she radiated sensuality. Her blond hair and velvety skin gave her a doll-like appearance, but any resemblance to a child's toy vanished when she walked across the carpet with that teasing sway of her hips.

In this apartment, she glowed like a golden candle.

Until he'd tried to see it through her eyes this morning, he hadn't realized how dark the place was.

Since Nora left, Jean-Luc hadn't felt much like opening the curtains. Now he wondered if, without realizing, he and the kids had remained in a state of mourning.

He could, he supposed, pick up some new curtains at a garage sale. There was always one going on somewhere in the neighborhood. And it wouldn't hurt to add a few more lamps and perhaps a painting or two.

But he didn't want to get carried away. Sandra probably wouldn't be around long enough to notice the difference.

The thought gave Jean-Luc a twinge in the region of his chest. All that driving yesterday must have strained his muscles.

"Let's go downstairs. The kids are at Ruthanne's," he said, without bothering to explain further.

"By all means."

Sandra strolled ahead of him into the sunshine. At his height, Jean-Luc got an excellent view of her hat with its unfortunate roses and a now cockeyed shepherdess.

To his surprise, he realized that he wanted to regain the money not only for himself and the children, but for Sandra as well. Why shouldn't she enjoy her opera galas and charity balls? Besides, once she resumed her life, sanity would return to his.

With it would come a normal pulse rate and the likelihood of a good night's sleep. And that, Jean-Luc told himself firmly, would be a very good thing.

ONCE SHE REACHED the foot of the stairs, Sandra hung back and let her husband go ahead. She had a hard time imagining how she would take care of children, or even what to say to them.

Did their father intend to inform them that he and Sandra were married? But if so, how would he explain their imminent divorce?

Perhaps he would go back on his word and introduce her as their grandmother. Oh, dear; she really was that, wasn't she? One could cease being a stepmother with the thump of a judge's gavel, but one never stopped being a grandmother.

Like it or not, these children were permanently related to her. She would have to invite them to visit at Christmas. Provide birthday presents. Remember to send a gift at graduation. Perhaps even stage the little girl's wedding at her home in Bel-Air.

Come to think of it, there were definite possibilities. One could build an entire season of entertaining around one's grandchildren, with appropriate ice sculptures, catering and orchestras. Sandra wondered what the likelihood was of persuading them to be bar and bat mitzvahed.

No sooner had Jean-Luc finished knocking than the door was opened by a thin woman of about fifty, who appeared to have been assembled on an off day. Her body was all joints and angles, and her waistline seemed to have ascended to the middle of her rib cage. She was of medium height, with salt-and-pepper hair and an amazing amount of makeup around her eyes.

"Ruthanne, I'd like you to meet Sandra," Jean-Luc said. "Sandra, this is Ruthanne Grover."

"Oh! Mrs. Duval! What an honor!" The neighbor executed a bob of the sort rarely seen outside of Queen Elizabeth's court. It went oddly with her patched shorts and stretch top.

"I'm pleased to meet you." When Sandra extended

her hand, she feared momentarily that the woman might kiss it. After the briefest of pauses, however, they shook.

"Dad?" A little boy peered from beneath Ruthanne's arm. "Who's this?"

"Your, uh..." Jean-Luc swallowed hard. "Stepmother."

"Stepmother?" cried Ruthanne. "You mean the two of you...? I can't believe it! You and Mrs. Duval got married? And I didn't even know until two days ago that you were related to *those* Duvals. But isn't she... I mean...*your* stepmother, Mr. Duval?"

"We stepmothers are creatures of infinite capacity," Sandra assured her. "Once we assume the mantle, we can serve an unlimited number of people."

The little boy stared with huge, purple eyes. He had dark hair, which must have come from his mother, and a pixielike face, which probably came from being six years old.

"Sandra," Jean-Luc said formally, "I'd like you to meet my son, Christian."

The moment had come. She wanted to say something welcoming but not effusive, meaningful but not affected. "Christian?" Sandra repeated. "How sweet, Jean-Luc. Your wife must have been religious."

An expression of astonishment crossed his face. "Not exactly. He's named after Christian Dior." Another small face poked from beneath Ruthanne's remaining arm. "And this is my daughter, Chanel."

Chanel was a paler version of her brother. She clutched a stuffed dinosaur close to her face, as if ready to duck behind it. "How do you do?" said Sandra.

"We're fine, thank you." Christian stepped forward and inspected her. "Are you really our new mother?"

"Only on a temporary basis," Sandra said.

"That means she's not staying," added Jean-Luc.

"Oh, dear." Ruthanne's mouth drooped. "I was so hoping...but of course, this is hardly the sort of place... I'm such an admirer of yours, Mrs. Duval."

Sandra hadn't been aware that she had any admirers, other than the maître d's whom she tipped generously. "Why, thank you."

"I've watched you on television." Ruthanne sighed. "You simply exude glamour. Just imagine, Sandra Duval, right here on my porch!"

The dinosaur inched forward until it blocked Chanel's face. In a high squeaky voice, it said, "What does 'exude glamour' mean?"

"It means she's like a movie star," said the little boy. "Doesn't it, Dad?"

"Yes, Chris, and right now the movie star is going to fix lunch for both of you." Jean-Luc scooped up his son and plopped the boy atop his shoulders. "Up we go!"

Ruthanne propelled the little girl forward. "If you have any problems, just call me."

"I certainly shall." Sandra wasn't sure whether she was expected to place the little girl onto her own shoulders, but she was afraid she might drop the child on the stairs. Besides, she knew so little about scooping and plopping. "What is your dinosaur's name, dear?"

"Fluff Nose," squeaked the stuffed animal.

"Shall we go upstairs, Fluff Nose?"

"Okay," came the high voice.

A few minutes later, Sandra found herself seated on the lumpy couch between the twins, with a stuffed animal on her lap and Jean-Luc headed out the door. It was every socialite's nightmare.

She contemplated various conversational openings and rejected them all. The boy seemed forthright enough, but she had no idea how to address the little girl, particularly since all comments apparently had to be filtered through the dinosaur.

"Excuse me," said Sandra. "I need to use my favorite appliance." They stood up at the same time she did. "Don't you two want to go and play?"

"We're hungry," whined the dinosaur.

Matters were deteriorating rapidly, she thought, and went to call Belle, as the twins trailed behind her.

CHANEL HAD DONE a lot of thinking about mommies. She liked the ones she saw on TV, but they were make-believe.

She liked her friends' mommies too, but they were already taken. Sometimes she thought of Ruthanne as her mommy, but she was more like a grandmother.

Chanel's own mother had left when she was three, and never even called. Maybe she'd died and Daddy hadn't told them because he didn't want to make them cry. Anyway, Chanel couldn't remember her, although Chris said he could.

She'd never met anyone like Sandra. Sandra was awfully pretty and smelled nice and had hair like a model on television. Chanel wasn't sure whether a lady like that could be a mommy, but she hoped so.

On the phone in the kitchen, Sandra said silly things like, "Peanut butter and jelly with bread? No sprouts? Oh, my gosh, Belle, this peanut butter has lumps in it! What do you mean, it's *supposed* to?"

Then, while they were eating, Sandra talked to Fluff Nose as if he were real, and pretended to feed him crumbs. She didn't tell stories about having a stuffed animal when she was a kid, either, which grown-ups sometimes did to try to make Chanel feel that they understood her.

Afterward, the twins washed the glasses and plates in the sink with a whole lot of soap. The bubbles got everywhere and Chanel kept dropping the plates. Sandra acted amazed that they didn't break, as if she'd never seen plastic dishes before.

Then she said, "Belle told me to take you to the park this afternoon. What does one do at the park?"

"Run around," said Chris.

"Feed the ducks in the lake." Chanel nearly forgot to talk through Fluff Nose and had to add a yip at the end.

"There's a lake?" Sandra brightened. "I could work on my tan. Oh, dear. I'll need a bathing suit *and* a disguise."

They pulled a box of Halloween stuff off a shelf and dug through a trunk of Mommy's old clothes. By the time they finished, Chanel was wearing a witch's hat, a pink tutu and black rain boots. Chris picked a yellow hard hat with a miner's light in front, and a knee-length T-shirt of Daddy's that advertised race cars.

Sandra's leopard-print bikini made her look like Sheena of the Jungle. That wasn't enough of a disguise, so she put on a loosely woven straw hat and a pair of pink heart-shaped sunglasses.

"If the *Enquirer* sees me, I'm dead," she said with a grin, and led the way out the door.

IT WAS FIVE-THIRTY by the time Jean-Luc arrived back at the apartment. He hadn't heard from Marcie all day—not that he'd had time to dwell on the subject.

Every car and half the trucks in Corona seemed to have overheated or broken down. There hadn't even been a spare moment to tinker with the prototype helicopter.

He was hot, sweaty and patched with oil. What he needed was a cool drink and a shower.

Surprisingly, that was what he got. The kids and Sandra were nowhere in sight. Since it was still full daylight outside, that fact didn't bother Jean-Luc until, freshly scrubbed and getting hungry, he realized that his wife probably didn't own a watch.

Besides, with no car, where could she have gone? He checked at Ruthanne's, but she hadn't seen or heard from his family all afternoon.

He'd never been the worrying type. But his kids had never disappeared before, either, Jean-Luc reflected as he got into his four-wheel drive and set off to cruise the neighborhood.

He frowned as he scanned the front of a convenience store. Two ponytailed men in black leather vests quaffed beer as they perched on the bumper of a truck. He could just imagine how they would react if Sandra sashayed by, all blond curls and feminine curves.

Darn it, he didn't want to think about his stepmother. Or wife, or whatever she was. He just wanted to find his kids.

When he came alongside the park, Jean-Luc remembered that the children liked to play here. He parked and got out. Several small rises and a smattering of trees blocked his view of the park's interior, so he strode into the green depths.

His first clue to what lay ahead was the sight of two old men on a rise opposite him, standing on a bench to get a better view. His second clue was the sound of children's voices shouting, "Quack! Quack!"

Jean-Luc quickened his pace. He could only imagine that the twins had escaped their stepmother's custody and come here by themselves, because he couldn't picture the social queen of Los Angeles cavorting in a neighborhood park.

If she had allowed his children to run around unsupervised, he would boot her pretty rear end all the way back to...

He came into view of the pond. It was a greenish blotch, not much bigger than a backyard swimming pool. Near the center, Sandra stood waist-deep with her back to him, arising from the water like Botticelli's Venus. Except Venus hadn't worn a leopard-print bikini or a straw hat that was doing its best to unravel before his eyes. She hadn't had a stuffed dinosaur pinned to her hat, either.

In the murky water, among the ducks, Chris and Chanel floated on their backs. His daughter's tutu was soaked, and so was his son's oversize T-shirt and shorts. The crazy woman had let them swim in their clothes.

"Quack! Quack!" the children yelled, and then Chanel sank and came up spluttering.

"You forgot to keep your head back!" Sandra commented in a high, squeaky voice, pretending that Fluff Nose was speaking. "Try it again!"

Obediently, Chanel flopped onto the water. This time, she managed to float alongside her brother.

It was one thing for an adult to play along with the child's dinosaur fetish, Jean-Luc thought. It was another thing to have Fluff Nose give the kids swimming lessons in a pond.

On the bench, one of the men wiped his spectacles and fixed them firmly back in place. When Sandra turned to keep track of the children, Jean-Luc got an eyeful of what the geezer had been staring at.

Her face might be hidden beneath a ridiculous pair of Lolita sunglasses, but only two wisps of fabric covered the rest of Sandra, and those wisps were stretched to capacity.

Last night, he'd been aware of her slender legs, but the rest of her had been hidden by Marcie's pajama top. He hadn't realized how delicately her waist nipped inward, or how straight her shoulders were or—how could a man not notice?—the roundness of her breasts, firm and full beneath the bikini bra as if daring a man to strip it away.

There she stood, half-naked for all the world to ogle. Including two men old enough to be her grandfather!

Jean-Luc stalked down the slope to the pond. At his approach, the children whooped and splashed their way into upright positions.

"Well, hello!" cried Sandra. "Taking a break?"

"A break?" he snapped. "It's six o'clock!"

"Really?" Sandra gazed around accusingly. "Well, someone should have told me!"

"Who? Those men with their eyes popping out of their heads?"

"What, those old fellows?" she said. "Aren't they cute? But they keep falling off the bench. I'm afraid one of them will get hurt."

"Hi, Daddy!" called Chris. "Sandra's teaching us how to swim!"

"She took Fluff Nose down the slide!" Chanel added, gesturing toward a playground faintly visible through the bushes. "He liked it!"

The kids waded toward a pile of shoes and hats on the bank. "And we dug a great big hole in the sand, almost to China!" said Chris.

"Some other kids helped us," announced Chanel. "And a dog, too. He digs pretty good."

Jean-Luc was on the point of correcting her grammar

when he realized that, for the first time in months, his daughter had spoken in her own voice. Before he could absorb that fact, Sandra herself reached his side.

"Your children are delightful." He wished he could see her eyes through the heart-shaped sunglasses. "We've had a splendid time!"

He sighed. What was the point of upbraiding them? The children hadn't been in any danger, although he doubted the water in the pond was particularly clean. "Next time, maybe we should discuss their agenda in advance."

"Lovely!" Sandra scooped up a towel, with which she proceeded to dry the children and herself. "Hats, everyone? Can't forget those! Are you walking back with us, Jean-Luc?"

"Walking?" Then it hit him. His wife and his children had strolled to the park in exactly the outfits they were wearing now. Sandra had paraded her bikini-clad body past whatever biker types were hanging out at the convenience store, past male motorists, past...

It didn't bear thinking about. Instead, he said, "We aren't walking. We're driving."

"Can we get take-out food?" asked Chris with his usual presence of mind.

Jean-Luc agreed. For once, he couldn't even think about dinner.

He was too busy wondering whether Sandra really planned to sleep on the couch, and how he was going to survive another night near those tempting curves, now that he had a very detailed picture of what they looked like.

5

THE RITUAL of eating dinner together in the kitchen, amid paper bags and plastic-topped cups spiked with straws, came as a novelty to Sandra. She hadn't done this in years; it made her feel like a teenager again.

Then she helped Jean-Luc bathe the twins and tuck them into bed. She didn't even mind reading aloud in Fluff Nose's high-pitched voice.

It astonished her that these squirmy, independent little creatures turned into clinging vines the moment there was a mention of lights-out. Chanel positively stuck to Sandra, her little arms as tight as stretch straps.

"I'll be here in the morning," Sandra promised.

"Really? Honest? You promise?"

"I won't go anywhere without telling you."

At last the children settled down. Firmly, Jean-Luc escorted Sandra out of the room.

"Maybe I should sit with them until they fall asleep," she protested as they reached the living room.

"You'll spoil them," he said. "Besides, if they get used to being coddled, what will they do when you're gone?"

"What did they do when Nora left?" she asked.

His expression grew shuttered. "Cried," he said tersely.

"It must have been awful. How long ago was that?"

"Three years."

That was half the kids' lifetimes ago, Sandra thought, and did some mental arithmetic. Malcolm must have died about a year before the twins were born; they hadn't even been conceived yet.

Had he known of his grandchildren, Malcolm would never have disinherited them. He certainly wouldn't have signed a will with such a harsh provision, preventing her from helping the little guys. It was all the more reason to hunt Rip Sneed to the ends of the earth.

She settled onto the sofa, surprised at how worn out she felt. What had she done today, after all? There hadn't been a charity fashion show to organize, or a promotional campaign to design for *Just Us*, or even a meeting of any of the boards of directors on which Sandra served.

She wondered if anyone missed her. Other than Belle, she doubted it.

There was no point in not being ruthlessly honest with herself. To the high and mighty of Los Angeles, it was Sandra's money that counted. Without it, she was just a high-spirited no-longer-quite-so-young woman who hadn't even finished college.

Her fling as Queen of Society had been fun while it lasted. Today had been fun, though, too.

"Tell me something," said Jean-Luc as he angled himself across an overstuffed armchair. "Why do you wear those fancy hats?"

As long as she was being honest with herself, Sandra decided to be frank with him, too. "When I first married Malcolm, I felt as if I vanished into the woodwork around his friends."

"The hats made you feel bigger?" He watched her from beneath half-closed lids.

"Exactly. Then I discovered that hats could be a form

of communication. Romance, humor, even satire. No one took them seriously, so I could get away with anything."

Leaning back against the pillows, she smoothed out the designer sundress she'd found in a trunk. Nora had good taste, Sandra had to admit. Expensive taste.

Jean-Luc had been frowning ever since he collected her and the kids at the park, but now his expression warmed. "The newscasts always focus on them. I remember the *Gulliver's Travels* hat you wore to the University Regents' Awards dinner with Dad."

"I just loved those cute little Lilliputians."

"Did you?" he murmured. "That book also satirized intellectuals who lose touch with reality. Are you sure you weren't tweaking the Regents just a bit?"

Sandra grinned. "And nobody figured it out! I got away with it!"

He smiled back, the expression transforming the hard lines of his face. Had he been sitting closer, she would have instinctively reached out to touch him.

It wouldn't be the first time today she'd had the urge to run her hands over some portion of that powerful masculine body. The man was delicious.

Briefly, Sandra contemplated marching across the living room—if one could march so short a distance—and perching on his lap just to see what happened. Technically, she knew what would follow. Emotionally, however, she couldn't understand why she should be so fascinated by the prospect.

Jean-Luc was handsome, but Los Angeles was full of good-looking men. Besides, the human mating act had a great deal more appeal to males of the species than to females, in Sandra's experience.

Although she had loved Malcolm, their marriage hadn't involved any blaze of passion. Looking back on it, she could see that she'd simply fallen into the relationship. That wasn't surprising. She often fell into things, and sometimes onto them or over them.

She had definitely stumbled into Jean-Luc. Together, they would achieve their mutual objective of nailing Rip Sneed to the wall and then stumble off into the sunset, separately.

So why did she keep wondering how Jean-Luc's mouth would feel pressed against hers? Why did she imagine him throwing her across the bed?

"Didn't the age difference ever bother you? Between you and Dad?"

Guiltily, Sandra wondered if he could read her thoughts, and then reassured herself that of course he couldn't.

Certainly the man wouldn't be thinking along those lines himself. As far as Jean-Luc was concerned, Sandra told herself, she remained his unwanted stepmother, the fortune hunter who had stolen his father and his inheritance.

"Because he was forty years older than me?" she said. "Malcolm was very handsome at sixty. Distinguished."

"But when you were thirty, he would have been seventy," Jean-Luc pointed out. "By the time you turned forty, he would have been—"

"At the time I got married, I couldn't imagine turning thirty," she said, then added, "I still can't picture myself at forty. I suppose it's inevitable, though, unless hard work kills me." She sighed. "We simply have to get that money back. Otherwise, one of these days, I might have to get a job."

"How are we sleeping tonight?" he asked abruptly.

The subject was not unexpected, but Sandra hadn't come up with any brilliant solutions. The couch was simply too short and lumpy. She had contemplated bunking with Chanel and putting Chris with his father, but she sensed that neither of the twins would sleep well and, as a result, neither would the grown-ups.

"We'll have to bundle," she said.

"Bundle?"

"It's an old New England custom. We did a special section in *Just Us* once on bedtime fads and follies over the centuries," she said. "We both wear our clothes, and we put something down the middle, like a rolled-up sleeping bag."

"If I had a sleeping bag," he said, "I'd sleep in it."

"We could roll some of your ex-wife's clothes and put them between us," she said. "That would be appropriate symbolism, don't you think?"

He regarded her with reluctant admiration. "And people don't think you have a brain in your head."

"They may be right." She shivered, remembering the lecture he'd delivered on the way home about the possible contaminants in the pond. "If the kids and I come down with the creeping crud tomorrow, it'll be my fault."

"I'll remember that," he growled. "You look exhausted. Let's go build a symbolic wall, shall we?"

To her disappointment, he headed down the hallway without waiting to take her arm. Sandra knew it was tempting fate, but she wished he would touch her, just a little.

TWO ASPIRIN and three cups of coffee barely got Jean-Luc through the next day. He ached all over, and the one place where he didn't feel stiff and sore, he just felt stiff.

Years ago, when he and Nora had slept in that bed, she'd complained about how small it was, but he hadn't noticed. At the time, young and supple, he'd enjoyed the chance to snuggle against his wife.

Now he understood how difficult it must have been for her. Nora, he'd later realized, hadn't enjoyed bodily contact. He had the opposite problem with Sandra: he wanted contact, ached for it and dreamed of it, but he knew it was vital to avoid it.

They'd wadded up his ex-wife's clothes, the ones that Sandra didn't think she would use, and stuffed them into a trash bag to form a divider. During the night, the bag had changed shape and the clothes had migrated, forming disconnected lumps instead of a unified barrier.

To make matters worse, Sandra was a restless sleeper. She murmured, she sighed, she rolled and she arched. It was the arching that had nearly done him in, especially when the movements pressed her soft places against his increasingly hard ones.

Jean-Luc had finally dozed in the early-morning hours, only to experience a sweaty dream in which he cornered Sandra in a hayloft. One garment at a time, she had stripped away her clothes and then his, but just as they'd rolled behind a barrel and he was poised to consummate their passion, the alarm went off.

All day, while he changed spark plugs and oil until his skin gleamed with grease, fantasies of Sandra tormented Jean-Luc. He recalled the edge of her mischievous smile and the way her navel seemed to wink as she stood in the pond. It was a wonder he didn't scald or scar himself.

His life would be better after she left, he told himself. Or it would be horribly, miserably empty.

In desperation, he trained his thoughts on his absent cousin. Where was she, and what was she doing? He tried several times to call her, but she wasn't answering her cell phone.

When the last customer had collected the last car, he locked the garage and walked next door to the ramshackle building where he'd built the prototype helicopter. There was nothing more Jean-Luc could do until he secured the rights to the material, but it always thrilled him just to look at it.

The spare building wasn't large, despite containing both the minicopter and his welding equipment. The point, after all, was to build a bird that could be kept in the average garage.

Jean-Luc found his throat tightening as he unlocked the side door and fumbled inside for the switch. His validation as an inventor and his children's economic future lay in this musty building.

Overhead lights crackled to life, bathing the crowded space with a flat glare. Workbenches, welding torches and other equipment surrounded the star of the show.

The little chopper perched proudly on the cement floor, its metallic surface gleaming. It was as beautiful as ever, Jean-Luc thought as he moved toward his creation.

About the width of an average car, it could carry roughly six hundred pounds—three average adults or two adults and two children. It was no substitute for the family van, but the vehicle's primary use would be long-distance commuting.

The retractable rotor was set flush into the top. Wheels underneath enabled the vehicle to taxi from its landing site into a garage or parking place.

It wasn't perfect, Jean-Luc reminded himself. The craft's lightness made it unsafe to fly in high winds, but he was already doing preliminary design work on a slightly larger and heavier version.

But unless he secured the rights to the material, he would remain one of those backyard inventors whose dreams of glory turn to dust. And Malcolm would be proved right.

Jean-Luc wondered what Sandra would say if he offered to take her aloft. It surprised him to discover that he didn't want to find out.

Suppose, like his father, she assumed he was wasting his time on pipe dreams? That he didn't have the talent to build anything innovative that was also practical?

Lots of people feared flying in helicopters and small planes, he reminded himself. Even if Sandra refused to go up, it wouldn't necessarily mean she mistrusted his invention. But it would bother him, all the same.

Anyway, he was too tired to take the bird out. Grumpily, Jean-Luc retreated into the small, gritty bathroom to shower. Usually he cleaned up at home, but he didn't want to appear in front of Sandra in his filthy state.

As he washed, he thought over the developments of the past day, or rather, the lack of developments. If Rip Sneed wasn't caught soon, he might sneak out of the country. Maybe he'd left already.

Furthermore, if Marcie didn't turn up, it might mean she was in trouble. Jean-Luc and Sandra needed to make some decisions about how to proceed.

He dried off, threw on a clean shirt and jeans, and headed for home. As he drove, an image of yesterday's discovery at the pond flashed through his mind. Whatever Sandra had done with the kids today, he hoped it didn't involve anything that would once again sear her half-naked body into his memory bank.

Outside the apartment, Jean-Luc spotted a familiar beat-up Toyota and felt a surge of relief. For good or for ill, Marcie was back.

She might have come to inform them that Rip Sneed was beyond their grasp. Or, conversely, that they had their hands on at least part of the money, and Sandra could leave. He didn't know which prospect alarmed him most, but he was glad his cousin was safe.

Upstairs, the apartment door stood open. Since that was the only way to get cross-ventilation, it didn't surprise him, but the sound of raucous laughter was unexpected.

Jean-Luc mounted the stairs quietly. He felt a childish impulse to check out what was going on before anyone spotted him. Slipping into the doorway, he looked inside.

The laughter, coming from the hallway, was superseded by the tootling sound of an imitation kazoo. It sounded as if Sandra was trying to play the "Grand March" from *Aida* by blowing through her fists.

The fanfare was joined by a series of clangs and thumps. And here came the parade.

Sandra emerged first, hands forming a mock trumpet in front of her lips. A teddy bear decorated her cloche hat, and she wore a gold-sequinned 1920s-style flapper gown that Nora had purchased for an outrageous amount of money. She gave Jean-Luc a wink and passed him without breaking step.

Behind her came Chanel in a pink Sunday dress. On her head sat a fake-flower-bedecked file folder, hole-punched and laced with ribbons that tied under the chin. As she walked, she banged a spoon against a xylophone.

The third marcher surprised him. He'd never seen Ruthanne Grover wear anything but spandex pants and stretch tops, except maybe at Christmas, when she changed into a glittery red-and-green T-shirt.

She had donned a braid-trimmed knit suit, also from Nora's stash. The demure shell and jacket hid the odd angles of her figure and gave her a businesslike air. It reminded him that Ruthanne had once been a secretary, before a combination of asthma and back trouble reduced her to temp work.

A makeshift pillbox hat, probably cardboard, was covered with striped contact paper. Atop Ruthanne's head it looked, well, less silly than it sounded.

Fourth in line came Marcie. She sported a short jacket over a hip-skimming dress of lavender silk that highlighted the color of her eyes. Her stick-straight black hair was gathered to one side in a French braid. The sophisticated effect was only partly dampened by the blue towel that turbaned her head.

The last one in line was Chris, beating a toy drum and wearing his soccer uniform and a baseball cap. He looked like a normal little boy, thank goodness.

The parade was wending its way toward the kitchen when Marcie noticed Jean-Luc. "Oh, hi!" His cousin blushed for the first time in his memory. "Sandra gave us a fashion makeover."

Ruthanne swung toward him, flustered. "I hope you don't mind...these clothes... I mean, they used to belong..."

To Nora, he finished silently. And he'd kept them all these years in a trunk, telling himself that Chanel might use them when she got older. But the truth was that he hadn't been able to bring himself to look at them.

The discovery that the woman he loved had only wanted his money had burned bitterly. There'd been other feelings, too, that he hadn't wanted to explore: the pain of first love betrayed, the anger at her abandonment of the children.

All that had been buried deep in a trunk that he couldn't bring himself to open. Seeing Sandra in a few garments hadn't bothered him, but he'd assumed it was because those particular items held no strong memories.

That wasn't true today. He could picture Nora quite clearly in the sequinned dress, dancing with him at a local nightclub. She'd intended to wear it to Malcolm's house as soon as they were invited.

As for the lavender dress, she'd bought it when she got the job singing in a nightclub. Only later had he realized that she had selected it to attract a new husband.

Today, Jean-Luc felt only the faintest echo of the dark feelings that had lurked inside him for so long. He wasn't even angry at Nora anymore. She had given him these children.

"I don't mind," he told Ruthanne, and meant it.

"Doesn't everyone look lovely?" Sandra's voice wafted back from the kitchen. "Look at Marcie's glorious eyes! And you never told me Ruthanne was a secretary. I may be needing one, you know."

"They look terrific." But Jean-Luc couldn't focus on anyone but his new wife. She carried off the gold flapper dress with a drop-dead sophistication that Nora could never have mustered.

The trick, he realized, was that Sandra's elegance came naturally. She transcended fashion. She had style.

After a few minutes, the parade disbanded and Ruthanne left. While the children continued marching and making noise, Marcie and Sandra whipped up a dinner of canned chili and corn. Then the three of them put the children to bed.

Afterward, they adjourned to the living room. "Maybe you'd better tell us why you're here," Jean-Luc said. "Have you found something?"

"Yes and no," Marcie said. "I thought we'd better discuss it in person."

"Shoot." He hated beating around the bush, especially when there was so much at stake.

"Sneed doesn't seem to be in Vegas any more." Although she'd changed into jeans and a tweed jacket, Marcie's hair was still twisted into the thick off-center braid. It gave her an almost exotic air. "The good news is, it doesn't appear that he gambled away the money."

"How do you know?" Still in sequins, Sandra lounged in a corner of the couch like Jean Harlow.

"I have a friend who works security for one of the casinos. He asked around." Marcie pulled out the photo that Jean-Luc had given her of their target. It was a good likeness of Rip, bald with beetled eyebrows, although it couldn't show his short stature. "No one's seen him, and I don't think he'd be easy to miss. Especially if he'd gambled away fifty million dollars."

"If that's the good news," Jean-Luc said, "what's the bad news?"

"He got thrown out of a motel because there were too many people coming and going," Marcie said. "They included a cameraman and a couple of sleazy-looking women who said they were actresses."

"So?" said Sandra.

"And then, the day after he left, two guys came looking for him." Marcie sighed. "The way the manager described them, you wouldn't want to run into them in a dark alley."

Sandra shook her head. "I don't get it."

"Somebody else is after him, too," Jean-Luc mused. He was sitting near the window, and the mention of the two thugs made him want to move away from it in case a bullet came through. He'd been watching too many gangster movies, he thought.

"You think he stole someone else's money, too?" Sandra demanded. "How could anyone be that greedy?"

"I don't think he stole money. More like—territory."

Marcie cleared her throat. "How much do you know about the mob?"

"He's poaching on the mob's territory?" Sandra's hands fluttered helplessly. "Goodness! But what do you think he's doing?"

"The camera, the women, that suggests..." Jean-Luc couldn't bring himself to finish the sentence in the presence of a lady. Two ladies, he amended, although he'd always pictured Marcie as one of the guys.

"X-rated movies," Marcie finished for him. "*Very* X-rated."

Sandra gasped. "Dirty pictures? Rip Sneed has been exploiting women with my money?"

"It's possible," said Marcie. "This brings up another matter for consideration."

"Which is?" Jean-Luc muttered.

"I realize it may take the police a long time to track Rip down, and the odds of their recovering the money are not good," said his cousin. "On the other hand, they're not likely to get shot by Mafia goons while they work."

"And you might be?" His wife leaned forward anxiously. "We can't have you running that kind of risk."

"You're withdrawing from the case?" he asked.

"Of course she is!" said Sandra. "She's done more than enough already. Thank you, Marcie."

He knew she was right, but suddenly the air in the room nearly stifled Jean-Luc. If he didn't come up with a few million dollars by the end of the month, he would lose the right to build his helicopter.

It wasn't worth risking Marcie's life. But it might be worth risking his.

"I'll take over from here," he said. "Just give me everything you have on Sneed."

"You're going after him? You could get killed." Marcie's eyes widened.

"Don't be silly," said Sandra. "We'll get this nonsense with the mob cleared up right away. I don't know why I didn't think of it before."

"Excuse me?" Jean-Luc eyed her as if she'd just proposed they bomb Las Vegas from his helicopter.

"Hal 'The Iceman' Smothers." She dug an address book from her purse. "You've heard of him. The one who built that new hotel."

Of course Jean-Luc had heard of him. Smothers was periodically indicted as the head of the West Coast crime family, but always managed to get the charges dropped before it came time for trial. "What about him?"

Sandra flipped through the book. "I'm sure Octavia Smith knows him. She used to be a starlet in the thirties and then she married a studio chief and now she's the grand old lady of the Hollywood aristocracy. Her daughter's been married about five times, to practically everybody. I think Hal Smothers was Number Three."

"I'm not letting you confront this man," Jean-Luc said.

"I wouldn't dream of it," said Sandra. "But I could arrange the meeting, if you like."

It didn't take more than thirty seconds to arrive at his answer. "I would like that," he said. "Very much."

6

JEAN-LUC LANDED the chopper on the helipad atop the Ice Palace Resort in Las Vegas. He'd made the two-hundred-and-fifty-mile trip in under two hours.

Score one for the MiniCopter.

A shiver of apprehension ran up his spine as, working almost by instinct, he retracted the rotors and taxied the bird to the refueling station. He scarcely noticed the admiring gazes of the heliport crew; he was too busy wondering what he was going to say to the head of the West Coast Mafia.

Mrs. Octavia Smith had been delighted to hear from Sandra. With one figurative crook of her finger, she'd arranged the appointment for the very next morning. There hadn't been time to dwell on what might happen, until now.

Jean-Luc didn't picture himself as an action hero. Despite his excellent physical condition from racquetball and swimming at the gym, he had no illusions about his abilities as a fighter.

On the other hand, he hadn't come here to duke it out with Hal Smothers. Especially not in light of the man's nickname. "The Iceman" was supposed to describe the way the man liked his drinks, but it more likely referred to his habit of leaving corpses behind on his climb to the top.

As Jean-Luc emerged into the desert sunshine, the staff

pelted him with questions. Where'd he get the bird? How much did it weigh? How fast could it move, how much had it cost, and what was it made of?

"Trade secrets," he responded to everything, and secured directions to Hal Smothers's office, leaving the men to gas up the bird for the return trip.

An elevator carried him down one story to the top floor of the hotel, which was reserved for executive offices. An attractive woman in a designer suit greeted Jean-Luc with a professional smile and escorted him down an oak-paneled hallway.

They crossed a plant-filled atrium in which parrots—bred in Petaluma, California, the woman informed him—squawked merrily beneath a glass dome, which, she said, had been custom-made in Pennsylvania. Just beyond it lay a dining room where a liveried staff was setting out champagne fountains and an ice sculpture of Cupid.

"Special doings today?" he asked.

"Oh, no," said his escort. "Just the usual luncheon for our executives. Mr. Smothers believes in nothing but the best. The champagne fountains were imported from..."

Jean-Luc stopped listening as they rounded a corner. He was too busy staring at the antechamber to Hal Smothers's office.

It might have been mistaken for an ancient temple. Beneath the soaring ceiling, larger-than-life-size marble statues lined the walls in a series of niches. Twin rows of chiseled pillars stood like sentries down the center, leading to oversize double portals.

"All the marble was quarried in Georgia specifically for Mr. Smothers," said the woman. "It was transported here in his private jets."

"Impressive," Jean-Luc said, although he was struck

more by his host's ostentation than by his taste. But then, the son of Malcolm Duval had grown up in surroundings every bit as luxurious as these.

At the far wall, his companion announced him into an intercom, and the double doors swung open by themselves. "Mr. Smothers will see you now."

Jean-Luc stepped inside. The doors shut behind him with a thud that reverberated through his bones.

"Mr. Duval!" On the far side of a giant space filled with ornate antique furnishings, Hal "The Iceman" Smothers arose from behind a desk the size of an aircraft carrier. He was a squarely built man, not quite as tall as Jean-Luc, with a thin white scar above his right eyebrow.

"Pleased to meet you." Jean-Luc strode across the patterned wool carpet and shook hands. Then, at a gesture from Smothers, he sat in a tapestry chair considerably smaller than the one occupied by his host.

"I heard on the news about what happened to your stepmother." Despite Hal's bland expression, his brown eyes were watchful. "Isn't it awful? You can't trust lawyers these days."

"Especially not Rip Sneed," said Jean-Luc.

"Naturally, I would like to help you catch the rat." Hal assumed an affable smile. "I would do anything for your stepmother. She's a lovely woman. Beautiful, beautiful. How is she, by the way?"

Jean-Luc had promised to say nothing about their marriage, in order to spare Sandra from prying questions once they split up. "She's holding up well. I didn't realize you knew her."

"Not personally." The Iceman's cheeks quivered, rodentlike, when he spoke. "I've seen her at the theater. Always wondered why Sandra didn't marry again. I suppose she didn't need to. But that's changed now, eh?"

"Excuse me?" Jean-Luc struggled to maintain an impassive air. Hearing his wife's name on this man's lips offended him.

"A classy dame like that needs a guy with bucks to take care of her," said Smothers. "Now that she doesn't have money of her own. Think she might be interested?"

His boldness startled Jean-Luc. Did the man expect Sandra to marry him sight unseen, just for his money?

He reminded himself that he'd had a similarly jaundiced view of her motives in marrying Malcolm until he got to know her. On the other hand, the very idea of Smothers's flat-knuckled hands touching her smooth skin, or those unreadable eyes gazing at her bare body, filled Jean-Luc with loathing.

With a start, he realized he was jealous. Pulse-poundingly, teeth-gnashingly jealous. What on earth was wrong with him?

"I'm afraid she's too upset about this Rip Sneed business to think about romance," he managed to reply.

From here on, he reminded himself, diplomacy would be vital. Smothers always hotly denied any connection to the mob.

"You, er, want somebody to go after this guy?" Interest flickered across the man's face. "You think Sandra would be impressed by something like that?"

"Somebody already is after this guy," Jean-Luc said. "Possibly someone of the criminal persuasion. Right here in Vegas."

"Really?" The gangster's eyebrows rose into twin peaks.

"My stepmother is afraid he might get wiped out before we figure out where he's stashed the money." Jean-Luc tried to weigh every word before it came out, but he was too distracted. He kept hearing the note of lust in the man's voice as he pronounced Sandra's name.

"So she would want this someone to back off?" Smothers said.

"Mostly she would like to know what Rip Sneed's involved in," Jean-Luc said. "And who, other than her, might want to kill him."

"She thinks I would know a thing like this?" He sounded on the verge of taking offense.

"Not you personally," Jean-Luc backpedaled. "But you're an influential man. No doubt you have a keen interest in keeping Las Vegas clean. So maybe you've heard something through contacts."

"The lady wants information." Smothers grimaced. "And I have none."

"Nothing at all?"

"As far as Vegas is concerned, Rip Sneed is not even a wart on a frog's ass," the man said. "If someone is trying to kill him, it must be a personal feud. Or maybe a man who wants to impress your stepmother. Such a thing I can imagine."

Jean-Luc uttered a long sigh. He believed Smothers was telling the truth; the man looked disappointed that he couldn't help. "Well, I know she's grateful that you agreed to see me."

"Tell her any time she wants to come visit, I will comp her the presidential suite," said Smothers. "Free room service, the works."

"I'll tell her." Jean-Luc stood. Smothers came around the desk to shake his hand, and walked him to the door.

The man was buttering him up, he realized. Already the hunter was laying his traps for an impoverished Sandra Duval. As if Jean-Luc would ever let her marry such a man!

He wasn't really jealous, he told himself. He just had an obligation to protect his stepmother while she was vulnerable.

SANDRA WAS GLAD she'd volunteered as a fill-in receptionist at the garage while Jean-Luc was gone. It wasn't so much that she'd needed a morning away from the children, who were darling but exhausting, or even that she wanted to make sure the customers understood that the boss would return later to take care of their vehicles.

Mostly, she wanted to be right here when he got back so she could see for herself that the Iceman hadn't shot him full of bullet holes.

Why, oh, why, had she ever trusted Rip Sneed? Why hadn't she taken charge of her own finances, regardless of Malcolm's instructions? She would never forgive herself if something happened to Jean-Luc when there was nothing more at stake than money.

The notion startled her. For one thing, fifty million dollars wasn't just money, it was a fortune. For another thing, she had no idea how she was going to live the rest of her life without it.

But then, she had no idea how she was going to live the rest of her life without Jean-Luc, either.

"Excuse me?" Sandra said aloud to the empty garage, where an Oldsmobile and a pickup truck sat dripping oil onto the already saturated cement floor. "Excuse me, who had that thought?"

A motor home dozing by the entrance refused to answer. So did the calendar on the wall, which, with a touch of Duval class, featured a cubist painting of a naked woman.

She peered into a cracked mirror stuck on the door of the cluttered office. "Did you think that?" Sandra demanded of her horror-stricken image. "Are you crazy? Of course you're going to live the rest of your life without what's-his-face."

She couldn't bring herself to pronounce his name aloud, as if the garage had ears and might repeat the story when he returned. It would be a disaster if Jean-Luc ever figured out that she was infatuated with him.

Infatuated. Now, there was a reassuring word. It described the intense but fleeting devotion of teenagers. Her feelings, too, would soon pass.

A whirr from outside caught her attention. With a surge of anticipation, Sandra hurried out of the garage.

Sunlight washed the summer sky stone-white. In the glare, a tiny point descended toward her, delicate as a hummingbird. It was strange to think that this toylike apparition had flown that great big man all the way to Nevada and back.

The chopper came down smoothly, with no jerks or hops. That probably meant Jean-Luc hadn't been injured, Sandra reassured herself. Maybe a black eye at the worst.

Oh, dear. What if Hal Smothers was now their enemy? On the other hand, what if he'd handed Rip Sneed over to them, signed, sealed and delivered?

The MiniCopter settled onto the concrete drive. Sandra jumped as a garage door churned open in the next building. It hadn't occurred to her that Jean-Luc would carry an automatic opener, just as in a car.

The blades retracted and the diminutive chopper rolled into the hangar, giving her a glimpse of the man inside. His face was partly averted as he concentrated on parking. She could read neither success nor failure in his expression.

Sandra dusted off her hands and went to meet him. She'd put on a pair of Armani pants and a checked shirt tied under the bust to reveal a bare midriff. Thank goodness for Nora's extensive wardrobe! Even the boots fit, although she didn't see the point of work shoes with high heels.

"Welcome back," she called.

Jean-Luc killed the motor and swung out of the copter. "So what do you think?" He gestured at the bird.

"It's terrific. Especially because it makes so little noise." At its loudest, it was no worse than a luxury car. "I'm sure there's a tremendous market."

He gave a tight nod. "But I haven't got a gopher's chance in a flood of ever putting it into production."

As he spoke, he pulled off his jacket and tossed it to Sandra. Unknotting the tie, he cast it toward her as well and began inspecting the whirlybird.

"That sounds like bad news." The jacket had a tweedy, masculine scent. Sandra tried not to inhale too deeply.

"Hal Smothers doesn't have a clue who or where Rip Sneed is." Jean-Luc spoke from a crouching position, checking the underside of the copter. "Whoever's after him, it isn't the mob."

"He actually admitted that?"

"Not in so many words. But we managed to make ourselves understood." Jean-Luc stood, impatiently brushing back an errant lock of hair. The gesture left a streak of oil on his forehead.

He reached for the first button on his pristine white shirt. "Be careful!" Sandra's warning arrived too late. Grease already smeared the collar.

Sunk in thought, Jean-Luc didn't appear to notice. He flung the shirt her way and strode toward the back of the building.

The arrogance of the man! But Sandra couldn't sustain

her annoyance. With his torso bare, she got a splendid look at those impossibly broad shoulders and the wide rib cage, tapering to a narrow waist and hips.

Classic, with just the right degree of bronzing. She wondered how he would respond if she walked over and blew lightly down the spine, from his nape to the tantalizing point where naked skin vanished beneath the belted slacks.

She never had time to find out. With a snap, the belt flicked out of its loops. At least the man had the sense not to throw it at her; he chucked it atop a nearby coatrack.

With a delicious sense of naughtiness, Sandra realized that a combination of distraction and habit had made Jean-Luc forget her presence. The man was changing into his work clothes without a thought for who might be watching.

She intended to take full advantage of the opportunity. He'd changed in the bathroom ever since they got married. She had a right to an eyeful; she was his wife, wasn't she?

Besides, she'd had to endure two nights of sleeping inches away from him. It was remarkable how many places a person could touch, and how much one could learn about masculine anatomy, simply by a bit of strategic tossing and turning.

In some ways, Sandra felt like an adolescent. She was insatiably curious about Jean-Luc. Much as she'd adored Malcolm, she'd never been intrigued by his body.

Jean-Luc was another matter. Right now, facing away from her as he stripped off the slacks, he was a picture of unconscious allure. Take those clinging black underpants, for instance. How did they manage to mold themselves so tightly to his butt that she could make out every curve and inlet?

She could almost feel their muscled hardness beneath her hands. The best position for that particular contact would be with him poised over her in bed, butt in the air, preparing to thrust into her with that essential, fascinating but still hidden portion of his anatomy.

With a sigh, Sandra watched him step into his work jeans. They were so caked with grease that they could stand upright by themselves. The show was over.

"What do we do next?" she asked. "Give the case back to Marcie?"

Jean-Luc paused in the middle of shrugging into his T-shirt. He turned sharply, his gaze flickering with astonishment as if he'd just become aware of her presence. "Give it back to Marcie?" he repeated.

"Now that we know the mob isn't involved," she said.

Frowning, he looked from her to his work clothes, then back again as if wondering how he'd managed to change without her noticing. Then he gave it up for a more productive line of thought. "I'm sure she'll work on it as her time allows. In the meantime, I'll arrange a meeting with Sam Orion."

"Who's he?"

"My friend who co-invented the material. I'll have to work out some other arrangement to get the rights."

Escorting her out, Jean-Luc flicked off the lights and closed the workshop. In the garage, he popped the hood on the Oldsmobile and began probing its innards.

Sandra didn't actually see any further oil or grease spray onto him. It just magically appeared, on a bulging bicep, on the back of his hand, across one cheek.

Soon he was covered with brownish-black blotches

and a healthy sheen of perspiration. The combination gave him a virile tang.

A picture of what he'd looked like moments ago, naked except for those minuscule black underpants, tantalized Sandra's memory. Her eyes could still trace the bulging muscles beneath the T-shirt and the inviting twitch of his rear end as he shifted positions beneath the hood.

How could the man be so gorgeous even when sweaty and soiled? Or, perhaps, *especially* when sweaty and soiled. If the place hadn't been so public, and his mind so obviously occupied elsewhere, she would have been tempted to suggest they close up shop for the day and consummate their marriage.

But to feel temptation did not mean one had to yield to it, Sandra reminded herself. There was a great deal to be said for self-control.

Just now, she couldn't remember what that great deal was. But she knew it would come back to her the moment she left his presence.

Jean-Luc was occupied in hooking the car to a monitoring device, so she went into the office and called Ruthanne to pick her up. When she returned, she surveyed the stained and cluttered garage, and wondered when it had begun to look so much like home.

Home. What was happening to her Bel-Air mansion right now? What strangers were digging through her possessions and muddying the rooms?

Rip Sneed was becoming more elusive than ever, and her chances of recovering her possessions were receding by the minute. More than that, it looked as if she and Jean-Luc might be stuck with each other for a long time.

The way things were going, they wouldn't even be able to afford a divorce. "Jean-Luc?" she said.

"Hmmm?"

"What if we never get the money back?"

He plugged something into something, cursed, and came up sporting another layer of oil. "We will. One way or another."

His mouth twisted grimly as a beat-up sedan chugged into the driveway, the engine spluttering and misfiring. Another customer. Another tedious job.

He couldn't bear to be stuck in this garage for the rest of his life. He had something to prove to himself, and to the memory of his father. More than that, his soaring imagination belonged in the clouds.

Sandra had never considered what she herself wanted from life. It hadn't been necessary, with Malcolm turning up when she was only twenty, offering a life beyond her wildest dreams.

She wasn't ready to decide what kind of future she wanted now, either. Somehow, things would work themselves out.

But Jean-Luc knew what he wanted. Turning the MiniCopter into a commercial success was his dream, and the only way to give it to him was to get her money back.

Thoughtfully, Sandra went outside to wait for Ruthanne.

7

CHANEL HAD BEEN worried all morning that Sandra wouldn't return. Chris kept bugging her to play Monopoly Junior, but she wasn't interested.

When Ruthanne said they were going to Daddy's garage to get Sandra, Chanel gave Fluff Nose a hug and burst into tears.

"Hey, what's with the waterworks?" Ruthanne bent down creakily. "Here's a tissue, sweetheart."

"I thought she wasn't coming back," Chanel said. "Like Mommy."

"Oh, honey." Ruthanne patted her head. "Sandra's not like... Well, I mean she wouldn't really... Not that she can stay forever."

"She can't?" Chris asked.

"I don't think so," Ruthanne admitted as she helped them put on their shoes. "She and your daddy are trying to get back some money. Then you'll be rich! Won't that be fun?"

"Can we have our own computer?" Chris said.

Chanel whapped him with Fluff Nose. "Who cares? I don't want to be rich! I want Sandra!"

Ruthanne gave her a sweet, sad expression, like a Raggedy Anne doll. "I'm sure she'd like that, too, honey, but it isn't that easy. Grown-ups can't just... I mean, things may look simple but... Well, we'd better not leave her standing on the sidewalk!"

All day, while Sandra helped them bake cupcakes and stage a party with paper hats for the stuffed animals, Chanel kept thinking about ways to make her stay. She thought about it through dinner. She thought about it at bedtime.

When the lights went out, she climbed up to Chris's bunk. "We need to talk about this money thing," she said.

He sat up and hugged his knees. "When we get the computer, I don't want you using it for girl stuff. If we're really rich, you can buy your own."

Boys were so dense! "It's about Sandra!" she said. "We have to make her stay, and I've been thinking. The trick is to make her fall in love with Daddy."

Chris pulled the covers around his chin. "Come on. How would we do that?"

"People always fall in love at parties." Chanel had watched a few romantic movies at Ruthanne's. "We have to get Sandra to throw one."

"Like today?" Chris asked. "That was fun."

"Not for stuffed animals! A party for grown-ups!"

"With ice cream?" he said, beginning to take an interest.

"And music!" she told him. "And dancing. And especially drinks. That's what makes people fall in love."

"What kind of drinks?"

Chanel tried to remember what the people had been drinking in the movies. "Well, they have these round glasses on sticks. Then they drink stuff that's kind of tan-colored."

"Like orange drink?"

"Orange drink is orange!" Considering that he was her twin, he could be awfully dumb sometimes. "Like ginger ale!"

Play "Lucky Hearts" and you get...

YOURS FREE!

This charming refrigerator magnet looks like a little cherub, and it's a perfect size for holding notes and recipes. Best of all it's yours ABSOLUTELY FREE when you accept our NO-RISK offer!

...then continue your lucky streak with a sweetheart of a deal!

1. Play Lucky Hearts as instructed on the opposite page.

2. Send back this card and you'll receive brand-new Harlequin Love & Laughter™ novels. These books have a cover price of $3.50 each, but they are yours to keep absolutely free.

3. There's no catch. You're under no obligation to buy anything. We charge nothing—ZERO—for your first shipment. And you don't have to make any minimum number of purchases—not even one!

4. The fact is thousands of readers enjoy receiving books by mail from the Harlequin Reader Service®. They like the convenience of home delivery...they like getting the best new novels BEFORE they're available in stores...and they love our discount prices!

5. We hope that after receiving your free books you'll want to remain a subscriber. But the choice is yours—to continue or cancel, any time at all! So why not take us up on our invitation, with no risk of any kind. You'll be glad you did!

The Harlequin Reader Service® — Here's how it works:

Accepting free books places you under no obligation to buy anything. You may keep the books and gift and return the shipping statement marked "cancel." If you do not cancel, about a month later we'll send you 4 additional novels and bill you just $2.90 each plus 25¢ delivery per book and applicable sales tax, if any.* That's the complete price—and compared to cover prices of $3.50 each—quite a bargain! You may cancel at any time, but if you choose to continue, every other month we'll send you 4 more books, which you may either purchase at the discount price...or return to us and cancel your subscription.

*Terms and prices subject to change without notice. Sales tax applicable in N.Y.

If offer card is missing write to: Harlequin Reader Service, 3010 Walden Ave., P.O. Box 1867, Buffalo, NY 14240-186

BUSINESS REPLY MAIL

FIRST-CLASS MAIL   PERMIT NO. 717   BUFFALO, NY

POSTAGE WILL BE PAID BY ADDRESSEE

HARLEQUIN READER SERVICE
3010 WALDEN AVE
PO BOX 1867
BUFFALO NY 14240-9952

NO POSTAGE
NECESSARY
IF MAILED
IN THE
UNITED STATES

"Ginger ale makes grown-ups fall in love?"

"Only if they're dancing."

"What flavor ice cream?" he asked.

Chanel knew he would never get his mind off the subject until she gave the answer he wanted. "Vanilla."

"My favorite!" said Chris. "Okay, let's tell Sandra we want a party."

"Let me think about it some more." Chanel climbed down. "We have to do this the right way."

"With chocolate syrup," said Chris.

ON SATURDAY MORNING, Sandra awoke with the sense that she absolutely had to find a way to make things happen. It was a wonderful feeling.

Ever since last Tuesday, when she'd lost all her money and turned thirty-two on the same day, she'd felt as if the world were rocketing out of control. Not any longer.

Today she was going to put her mind to finding a solution to their problems. One way or the other, they had to recover the money so Jean-Luc could manufacture his helicopters. Riding on a wave of optimism, Sandra had faith that nothing lay beyond her scope.

It might help as a first step, she told herself a few minutes later, if she could finally manage to make toast without burning it. The trouble was that Jean-Luc's toaster had died and she had to broil bread in the oven. One second on the wrong side of done, and it was Scorch City.

There had to be a better way. While Jean-Luc was getting dressed and the kids tiptoed around the apartment, giggling and whispering as if planning something, Sandra melted margarine in a large frying pan and fried the bread. Voilà! Not only unburnt, but prebuttered as well.

"Breakfast!" she called.

Everyone gathered around the table. Watching them eat, Sandra could feel the air humming with their thoughts.

Jean-Luc wore a half frown, his lips moving as if he were rehearsing a speech. She suspected he was preparing what to say to his friend Sam, who had agreed to meet him at the garage today.

The kids kept poking each other, catching each other's eye and nodding as if trying to spur the other to say something. It was Chanel who spoke first. "Do you like ginger ale?" she asked.

Sandra had learned that the children usually had a serious reason for even the silliest question, so she gave a serious answer. "It's not my very favorite, but it's on my top-ten list of soft drinks."

"How about dancing?" asked Chris.

Sandra couldn't see the connection between ginger ale and dancing, or why these would occasion so much whispering and giggling. "With the right partner," she said cautiously.

"How about Dad?" asked Chanel.

Jean-Luc emerged from his fog. "I haven't danced in years. Why?"

The little girl started to speak, gulped, and snatched Fluff Nose from her lap. With the dinosaur in front of her, she squeaked, "We want a party!"

"You're going to one today, don't you remember?" their father said. "One of your little friends is having a birthday. Josefina, isn't that her name? We bought a book for her and wrapped it last weekend."

Chanel and Chris exchanged looks of near panic. "Not that kind of party!" Chris said.

"The grown-up kind with ginger ale."

"Excuse me?" Jean-Luc stared at them blankly.

Seeing that Chanel was on the verge of breaking into tears, Sandra added hastily, "It's not a bad idea," although she had no idea how one could give a party in an apartment the size of a teacup. "Why don't we discuss it later?"

The children finished eating and hurried from the table. Their father watched them go with an expression of bewilderment. "What was that about?"

"I don't know," Sandra said. "But it's not a bad idea. Parties boost morale."

He made a grumping noise. If he'd been holding a newspaper, she was sure he would have rattled it. "I can just see it. You, me, Ruthanne, Marcie and Hal Smothers, waltzing around the living room."

"Why do you mention Hal Smothers?" she said.

"Well, we'd have to invite someone to help with the boy-girl ratio," Jean-Luc muttered. "And he'd probably come."

The man wasn't making any sense. "Why?"

"Didn't I tell you he's got the hots for you?"

"It must have slipped your mind." The head of the West Coast Mafia had a crush on Sandra? She'd never even met the man, unless you counted the time after an opera when he elbowed her out of his way while heading for the exit.

"He considers you fair game now that you're broke," Jean-Luc explained. "Let me see, how did he put it? 'A classy dame needs a guy with bucks to take care of her,' or words to that effect."

He excused himself to prepare for the helicopter ride he'd promised Sam, who had a pilot's license and wanted to try the craft for himself. Sandra got the kids ready to go to their friend's house, but ideas were yammering so loudly in her brain that she scarcely noticed what she was doing.

The news that The Iceman took an interest in her created all sorts of possibilities. Not that she had the least intention of contacting that thug.

But if he didn't consider her beyond the pale, maybe she wasn't as much of an outcast as she'd believed. Come to think of it, when contacted with a request, Mrs. Octavia Smith had been delighted to help. Maybe some of Sandra's other friends hadn't abandoned her, either.

As she brushed Chanel's hair and washed Chris's face, she thought about pals and parties and old-fashioned occasions where everyone brought food. The same God had created caviar and hot dogs, orchestras and boom boxes.

It wasn't so much that Sandra missed her old high-flying ways, although they did produce a certain nostalgia. It wasn't even that she wanted to thrill the kids, since she still wasn't sure why they seemed so gung ho about giving a party for grown-ups.

But it was just possible that among her wealthy acquaintances might be one with a passion for aviation and a few bucks in venture capital floating around. Well, okay, a few million bucks.

She would have to organize the event by next weekend at the latest. Belle and Octavia could help.

Sandra hummed to herself as she walked the kids two blocks to their friend's house. She was going to be busy, she could see that.

IT HAD BEEN YEARS since Sandra had ridden a bus. This one smelled of diesel fuel and sun-cracked vinyl. It jounced over every pothole with bone-crunching fervor.

Toward the front of the bus, a Hispanic lady was reading to her two children from *The Runaway Bunny*. An old man dozed on one of the benches, his snores ripping and snuffling in sync with the vehicle's movements. Across the aisle, two teenage girls in exercise outfits kept sneaking glances at Sandra.

She wore the lavender dress and short jacket that Marcie had modeled for the parade. The decorations had been removed from her white silk hat and replaced by strategically glued plastic figurines of Snow White and the seven dwarfs, borrowed from Chanel.

It was, Sandra supposed, an odd outfit to wear to a garage, but she did want to impress Sam Orion. Without his cooperation, the whole project would be lost.

Jean-Luc had called a short time earlier to report that his friend was dying to meet her. She'd finished the last of her phone consultations with Belle, changed clothes, and here she went.

She tugged an overhead line, setting off a small bell. The driver gave her a nod in the rearview mirror and pulled to the curb.

Brakes creaked. The old man sputtered and snorted in a rhythm vaguely reminiscent of the opening bars of "The Star-Spangled Banner." The teenage girls sighed as Sandra arose, smoothed the wrinkles from her skirt and sauntered down the aisle.

She was passing the Hispanic family when the mother finished the book. Snuggling against her, the little girl said, "I'll always be your little bunny."

The strangest thing happened. It was as if a giant fist closed over Sandra's heart and gave it a squeeze. She could barely pay attention as she finished traversing the aisle and went down the steps.

For some reason, the little girl brought Chanel and Chris to mind. Overlaid on the buildings around her, Sandra could see their curious eyes and morning milk mustaches.

Above the honk of a horn and the drone of a distant airplane, she could hear Fluff Nose squeaking. Over the scent of exhaust fumes, she smelled the potent mix of baby shampoo and teddy-bear fur.

She missed them. It was incredible, crazy, inexplicable. Of course Sandra *liked* these children—who wouldn't?

But now, unbelievably, she found herself worrying about them. Were they having a good time at the party? Would they remember to wash their hands before eating? What if the party broke up early and someone tried to call her, and she wasn't there?

She gave herself a mental shake. The children had gotten along just fine without her for six, nearly seven years. They weren't going to disintegrate because she spent a few hours away.

After walking half a block, she found that the garage was locked for the weekend but the hangar next door stood open. The MiniCopter had been left outside after its outing, but there was no sign of Jean-Luc.

A round-faced man adorned by freckles and thick glasses sat with the side door open and his feet sticking out of the bird. With his reddish crew cut, he looked like a refugee from *Happy Days*.

Sandra strode toward him, aware that her high heels gave her hips a feminine sway. A light breeze ruffled the silk of her hat, and she wondered what the Seven Dwarfs made of all this California sunshine.

"Sam Orion?" She extended her hand. "I'm Sandra Duval."

The man stood up so abruptly he bonked his head on

the curving doortop. "Oh! It's such a pleasure to meet you. Such an honor, I mean."

"Are you all right?" He'd made a pretty good thud. From the sound of it, he'd probably raised a lump.

"Fine. Everybody says I have a hard head." Only a few inches taller than Sandra, he stared at her with undisguised awe. "And you're such a vision! Even better than on television. I've never seen that hat before. It must be new!"

Good heavens, the man kept track of her hats? Didn't he have anything better to do? "Just a little something I threw together. Is Jean-Luc around?"

"He went to crunch a few numbers." The redheaded man gestured her into his former seat in the copter. "We're trying to figure out a way to get my partners to accept shares in his company in lieu of money up front."

"That sounds like an idea." But not enough of one, Sandra thought as she sat down. Even if the men contributed the rights to their material, she doubted they would provide the necessary start-up capital.

"So tell me how you came to discover this... this...what *do* you call it?" She reached out and tapped the metal exterior.

Sam stood straddle-legged, clasping his hands behind his back. "It's, uh, Cybermolecular Hypertonic Substrate, or Chyps for short."

"Chyps?" said Sandra.

"With a Y." Sam radiated eagerness to please.

"Wouldn't you prefer something more descriptive?" Success depended on image, and the right image depended on the right name, in Sandra's opinion. "Chyps sounds like a new kind of snack food. How about, say, TuffStuff?"

Sam chewed on his already well-gnawed lips.

"TuffStuff does have a nice ring. But I mean—'Stuff.' It's not very high-tech."

"How about Tufftech, then?"

"Tufftech," he repeated. "That's good. I'll suggest it to my partners."

Sandra adjusted her position demurely. "So how did you come up with it?"

"I was in my lab…" He launched into an explanation that involved two fellow researchers, an attempt to develop videotapes that wouldn't wear out or break, and an unexpected chemical reaction.

"And that's how it happened," Sandra murmured admiringly. "A sizzle, a funny smell, and you've changed the future. Just like Sir Alexander Fleming discovering penicillin."

Sam grinned so hard his freckles danced. "I never thought of it that way. You're so sharp! I can't believe I'm really talking to Sandra Duval! You know, you're even prettier in person. Your skin, why, it looks like velvet!" This was getting a bit personal.

"Mr. Orion," Sandra said, hoping to inject a note of formality by using his last name, "I hope you and your partners will come to my party next Saturday afternoon. Everything is finalized except the place."

"Me? Invited to a Sandra Duval party?" He stared at her.

"Due to my reduced circumstances, everyone is bringing a dish," she said. "What's your specialty?"

He responded without hesitation. "I make pretty good fried rice over a Bunsen burner."

"That should be interesting," she said.

Sandra sensed Jean-Luc's approach without turning. It was as if she felt a ripple in a force field.

Swiveling, she let herself relish the lean length of the

man. He was marching toward the copter, absorbed in a sheet of paper. Not until he had nearly reached them did he look up.

His stride broke, and a dazed expression crossed his face as if he couldn't figure out what she was doing there. Then he gave her a crooked smile. "Sorry I wasn't here to greet you. I've been running some numbers."

"Sam told me." She restrained the urge to walk over and slip her hand into his. No one was supposed to know they were anything other than stepson and stepmother. Besides, that really *was* all they were, in the long term, she reminded herself.

"I think we can work this out." Jean-Luc handed the sheet to his friend.

The man scanned it, blinking owlishly. "I'm sure it will do fine. Well, I'm not sure, but I hope so. It's just that they have a tendency to get greedy, and there's so much money to be made with—Tufftech. That's what Sandra suggested we call it. Have you told her about the possibilities?"

"I like the name, and it's worth billions," Jean-Luc said simply. "But all I'm asking is one tiny piece of the rights. They'll still be able to sell the rest to major corporations and the government."

"Insulation. Miniaturization. Medical applications," Sam added. "The list is endless!" He clutched the paper, not seeming to notice he was wrinkling it. "Well, I'd better be going. Thanks for the ride, J-L. Sandra, I'm looking forward to your party!"

"I'll call you with the details."

With a handshake and a wave, he loped off. Jean-Luc emerged from deep thought to say, "What party?"

"You remember the children's request." Sandra took a deep breath.

"Somehow I get the impression you aren't just having a few friends over for ginger ale." Where a few moments before Sam had jiggled and fidgeted, Jean-Luc stood like a rock. Not a very happy rock, either.

"Well…" She might as well confess everything. "I called my housekeeper at her home. Thank goodness she removed my personal papers and my computer disks for safekeeping."

"Computer disks?"

"You don't think I could run my life without a computer, do you?" she said. "Anyway, I had Alice—the housekeeper—fax the guest list from my birthday party to Belle at her office."

He managed a rueful smile. "High society goes high-tech."

"We've rescheduled it for next Saturday!" she said. "Belle and Octavia have called everyone, and a lot of them are coming. The only thing we haven't decided is where to hold it."

She could have sworn a trace of sadness darkened his violet eyes, but why should he feel bad about her resuming old friendships? "At this rate, you'll be back to normal in no time."

"Not quite, but things aren't as desperate as I feared," she said. "Belle's husband, Darryl, knows a lawyer who's agreed to represent me on a deferred-fee basis. He's blocked the foreclosure until the details of the embezzlement are sorted out. Isn't that wonderful?"

"Then you could return home now, if you wanted," he said slowly.

"And set the press on my tail?" It was the best explanation she could come up with for rejecting the idea, certainly better than admitting she was in no hurry to get away from Jean-Luc and the children.

It was a relief when he changed the subject. "You seem comfortable sitting in the bird. Care for a ride?"

Sandra didn't need any encouragement. "I'd love one."

He scrutinized her as if making sure she meant it. "You're not going to panic?"

"In your experience, do I panic easily?" she demanded.

"Not that I've noticed, but I haven't give you any reason to," he said.

"Other than kidnapping me?" she retorted.

He grinned. "All right, let's go."

Sandra had been expecting some preliminaries. An inspection of the aircraft. The ritual of donning a helmet and perhaps a space suit. "You mean right now?"

"Without further ado," he said.

"Okay." She swung her legs into the copter and fastened her seat belt.

Jean-Luc closed and locked her door and went around to the pilot's side. A moment later, the motor sprung to life.

Suddenly, in a dark rush of doubts, Sandra wondered what on earth she had let herself in for. When she was younger, she'd leaped at the chance to scuba dive with Malcolm. Skiing in Switzerland had been a breeze.

But now she was vaulting into the sky in a MiniCopter that looked like a fishbowl. Not to mention that it was made from stuff that had been invented accidentally by three guys trying to make better videotapes.

Sandra gripped the armrest as if she were hanging on for dear life, and kept her mouth firmly shut. She would sooner spin into the great beyond than let Jean-Luc know she didn't trust his greatest invention.

8

CAUGHT BY A GUST of wind, the chopper gave a little dip, and Sandra's stomach lurched. They were only a few feet above the driveway, and she calculated she could bail out without suffering more than a broken ankle.

A glance at the pilot showed him relaxed but alert as he lifted them further from Mother Earth. He worked those controls with cheerful intensity, as if he were flying a video game.

She'd ridden in a helicopter once before, island-hopping with Malcolm, but she hadn't paid much attention to the dashboard. How could anyone keep track of so many dials?

They swooped into the sky, and there was no longer any question of jumping. Not that Sandra had seriously considered it in the first place, but now she would break a lot more than an ankle.

The town below grew smaller. She felt isolated and tiny, buoyed by a bubble of air but rocked by every passing breath of wind. A primitive instinct made her want to demand what in heaven's name was holding them up.

"Nervous?" Jean-Luc asked.

"A little." She tried to loosen her grip on the armrests but her hands refused to cooperate. "I mean, we are kind of defying gravity."

"It's all a matter of lift." He shifted a lever and they swooped forward. "The shape of the wings makes the airflow over it in a way that creates less pressure above the wing than below. Therefore, we rise.''

"Obviously," Sandra said.

He chuckled. "It's the same principle that makes the wind blow. Elementary."

"Then why didn't people think of it a long time ago?" she demanded.

"They did," he said. "The Chinese wrote about it as early as 300 A.D., and Leonardo Da Vinci sketched a design for a helicopter. Models were built as early as two hundred years ago."

"I don't recall anybody whirlybirding around in the Victorian era," Sandra said skeptically.

"That's because the engines were too heavy," Jean-Luc said. "Helicopters weren't practical until the gasoline engine came along."

It was the confident tone of his voice as much as what he was saying, but as they angled south across the city, Sandra's fear ebbed. She found she actually enjoyed the freedom of movement.

There was no one else around, not at their level. Above and in the distance, she spotted a jet heading for Ontario International Airport, a dozen or so miles to the north. Below, she made out buses, cars and trucks chugging along on their earthbound way.

But here in midair, she and Jean-Luc reigned supreme. No roads restrained them; there were no speed limits and no dispatchers. They were creatures of the light, eagles soaring into the limitless vastness.

Below them, canyons unrolled. A canopy of trees spread across the land, reminding Sandra of how this entire region must have looked fifty years earlier. To the west, she glimpsed the suburban sprawl of Orange

County, but here they were still in the land of the mountain lion and the coyote.

Okay, she couldn't actually see any mountain lions or coyotes. But she could see a lone wolf, the one-of-a-kind airborne variety. Jean-Luc.

Just to watch his expression as he piloted the craft was to feel the joy radiating through him. His shoulders hadn't looked so broad and powerful since the day he abducted her in the limousine. He held his chin high, and a teasing smile played around his lips as if he were making love to the universe.

A shiver of desire ran through her as she watched his muscular arms and strong hands guiding the controls. Sandra could almost feel those arms encircling her, and see the same eagerness illuminating his face as he swept her into the bedroom.

But there her imagination failed. It was impossible to reconcile the pleasant but routine experiences she'd had during her first marriage with the fantasies that sent heat coursing through her body now.

"I've got to watch our location closely." He studied a computerized map on the instrument panel. "There are some military aircraft installations with restricted air space, and we're nearing the flight path for John Wayne Airport."

How dare anyone else encroach into their domain? Sandra wondered resentfully, and then smiled at her own indignation. She'd just discovered the joy of flying today, and then only because of Jean-Luc. The sky hardly belonged to her, yet she felt as if she owned it. As if they owned it, together.

"Are we going somewhere in particular?" she asked.

"I thought I'd make a sweep over the beach house," he said. "I want to see if there's any sign of occupancy."

"But Darryl's lawyer put everything on hold," she reminded him.

"All the more reason why Rip Sneed might be hanging out there," he said. "There's no risk of the bank sending anyone down, even if they have figured out that it's part of your holdings."

They hovered above the rooftops of Newport. Along the beach, Sandra could make out the copter's round shadow moving over the sunbathers.

She read fascination on people's upturned faces, although from this distance she might be imagining it. But surely they must be wondering about the small craft that made so little noise.

"There it is." Jean-Luc pointed toward the driveway where she'd stomped on his foot last Tuesday. Less than a week ago, Sandra thought in amazement.

No cars were parked in the driveway. After a first pass, Jean-Luc returned and they landed. "I'll just be a minute," he said as he hopped out.

He returned with a handful of flyers and junk mail. "If anybody's home, they aren't picking up the mail," he said, and they popped back into the air.

"It's perfect," Sandra said.

"Excuse me?" He steered above the coastal bluffs, back toward Corona.

"For my birthday party!" She clapped her hands. "There's hardly any furniture in the house, so it can hold lots of people. And the children could play on the beach!"

He didn't answer for a moment, and then he said, "Also, Newport is a prestigious address. Your friends will feel right at home."

Maybe he hadn't intended a dig, but Sandra felt her hackles rise. "My friends aren't snobs!"

"I didn't say they were."

"There are lots of down-to-earth people coming, like the staff of *Just Us*, and the people from Darryl's magazine, too." Belle's husband edited a magazine for single men. "Your apartment is too small, but if you'd rather, we could hold the party at your garage. Of course, it's a bit limited in the area of kitchen facilities, but Sam did say he cooks rice over a Bunsen burner."

"You invited Sam?"

"And Ruthanne and Marcie, of course. Jean-Luc, this is a party for all our friends!"

The corners of his mouth quirked, and she guessed that his prickly mood had passed. But all he said was, "You hardly know Sam."

"He's *your* friend," she pointed out. "You can invite whoever you like. Just tell them to bring a dish to share."

They had left the coastal regions and were passing above the canyons again. "You're telling me that Mrs. Octavia Smith is going to bring a covered dish?"

"Yes, and she's going to cook it herself," Sandra informed him. "She said she hasn't made blintzes since she was a bride. She's looking forward to it."

"So am I," said Jean-Luc.

THE EXCITEMENT had begun building inside him the moment he closed the door to the helicopter with Sandra inside. She was going up with him. She respected him enough to trust her life to his invention.

Even as he concentrated on his flying, Jean-Luc remained acutely sensitive to her body language. He felt her tension, and knew when it eased. He felt her gaze caress his arms and chest, and knew she was becoming aroused.

And so was he. Not just physically, but in ways he

couldn't name. It was as if they were tuned to the same frequency.

He'd never felt anyone else's emotions so keenly, except those of his children, and he definitely didn't think of Sandra as a child. She was all woman, every blond inch.

He didn't merely want to take her to bed. He wanted to explore her, and stimulate her, and laugh with her. He wanted long, languorous days beneath a tropical sun and even longer nights beneath a ceiling fan, with the nearby pounding of the surf forming a counterpoint to their lovemaking.

He had to do something before he became obsessed. He was very close to that state already.

Once they landed back at the garage, he let Sandra out of the chopper before rolling it into the hangar, on the pretext of preventing her from stepping in an oil puddle. After killing the engine, Jean-Luc sat behind the controls for a moment, trying to figure out an excuse to avoid going home with her.

A long evening awaited, and tomorrow the garage would remain closed all day. How was he going to spend two nights and an entire day in her presence without taking her in his arms and doing something they would both regret?

The answer was simple. He had to stay away as much as possible. It might be unfair to both Sandra and the kids to leave them alone so much, but it was the right decision.

He emerged from the garage and handed her the keys. "Take the car. I'll catch a bus later."

Blue eyes blinked at him. "But the shop is closed on Saturday."

"I need to check out the chopper," he said.

"It's that delicate?" she asked. "I mean, your average purchaser isn't going to be able to give it a daily tune-up."

The truth was that the copter didn't need attention, but Jean-Luc could hardly tell her that. "I need to make sure no flaws develop," he improvised. "Remember, I've tested the prototype thoroughly, but it is still new. As a matter of fact, I'm already planning to incorporate some design changes before we go into production."

"Really? What kind of changes?"

Was the woman deliberately putting him on the spot? he wondered, and then remembered that she had a fifteen-percent investment in his company. "I think I could make it a little more user-friendly."

Since she was watching him expectantly, Jean-Luc went to his drafting table and brought back a blueprint. He showed her a couple of engineering changes that would give the craft better stability and maneuverability.

Sandra studied the plans attentively. "Are you going to have to build another prototype?"

"Well, I was planning to wait until I had the funds to hire some..." He blinked a couple of times as her suggestion hit home. *Of course. Build another prototype now.* That would give him an excuse to spend tomorrow here, and every evening next week. "You know, you're right."

"About what?" she said.

"I've been thinking I should wait until I can pay a crew to help me," he said. "But even if Sam lands me the rights, I'll still be scrabbling for money. I should get started on the new prototype right away."

Dismay flashed across her face. "You work so hard as it is."

"I'm building a future for my children," Jean-Luc said. "It's worth it."

A long sigh escaped from her. "I thought at least we would have this weekend to, well…" She shrugged. "You're right. If you think the children can stand your absence, this might be the best thing."

"It is." Instinctively, Jean-Luc reached for his work clothes. He was on the point of unknotting his tie when he remembered that he'd been through this routine before.

Come to think of it, Sandra had been standing right there watching him undress the other day. How could he have forgotten himself like that?

He wouldn't make that mistake again. "You'd better relieve Ruthanne. I don't want to take too much advantage of her."

"Absolutely." Then Sandra's jaw dropped open. "Oh! They're not at Ruthanne's, they're at that birthday party! It was supposed to end half an hour ago!"

"You'd better hurry then," muttered Jean-Luc, although he hated to see her go.

Clutching the keys, Sandra started for his car. Halfway there, she turned and made a gesture as if starting to say something, but it turned into a wave.

For one self-indulgent moment, Jean-Luc lingered, watching her slim figure undulate across the parking lot. That lavender dress looked better on her than it ever had on Nora. But then, a lot of things did.

With a mental straightening of the shoulders, he turned toward the hangar.

IT WAS TUESDAY night when Sandra awoke around 1:00 a.m. and heard noises in the living room. Her heart lurched into her chest, until she realized it was Jean-Luc.

She'd hardly seen him since Saturday. He'd spent all day Sunday and part of Monday gathering parts to begin building the new helicopter. Today, he must have begun the actual construction.

During his forays, he'd acquired an army-surplus sleeping bag, which he unrolled in the living room and slept on at night. He'd said that this way he could come in late without waking her.

She missed him. The kids missed him, too. Still, she could hardly ask him to stay home when his work was so essential.

Besides, she had a sneaking suspicion that her presence was part of his motivation for staying away. Sandra had great faith in women's intuition, particularly her own. And it told her loud and clear that Jean-Luc's masculine desires were working overtime.

Maybe he would feel the same way if sharing an apartment with any attractive woman, Sandra reminded herself as she eased out of bed and ran a brush through her hair. From what little she knew of men, their desires were easily provoked, even by pictures in magazines.

She had no reason to believe Jean-Luc was any different. Also, with his fierce independence and his dislike of the wealthy world his father had inhabited, he surely had no desire to make their relationship a permanent one.

Neither did she, Sandra told herself as she belted a silky bathrobe over her nightgown.

She moved softly out of the bedroom and into the hall. Jean-Luc had left the living room dark, but had turned on a light in the kitchen.

He stood silhouetted in the doorway, drinking a can of soda. She could see the outline of his muscular torso and, when he shifted position, light gleamed across the bronzed surface of his skin.

A volcanic burst of desire swept through her. She measured the distance to him, the few steps it would take before her hands touched those slim hips and the slinky fabric of her robe brushed against his bare chest.

She had a distinct image of him catching her by the shoulders and slowly sliding to his knees, his mouth trailing along her breasts. Her nipples hardened at the thought.

Where did these feelings come from? Why did she experience them so intensely around Jean-Luc? She'd never felt this way when she was married, and certainly not since then.

Would it be so terrible if she yielded? Sandra felt almost certain that Jean-Luc wanted her as much as she wanted him. Other people had affairs and then went their separate ways. Why couldn't they?

Because once we pass the point of no return, we can never go back to being friends.

Nor could they go on to being a real husband and wife. The differences between them were too deep-rooted.

The ultimate pain wasn't worth a few nights of pleasure, Sandra admitted with a twist of sorrow. Still, it took all the strength she possessed to retreat down the hallway and return to bed, alone.

The vision of Jean-Luc standing against the light, stripped to his primal male essence, branded her thoughts and, for the rest of the night, her dreams.

ON SATURDAY, Sandra and the kids rode to the beach with Ruthanne so they could set up in advance of the party. Jean-Luc wanted to get in a few more hours of work on the prototype before joining them.

The craft had gone together with remarkable speed.

He'd had to buy parts for the engine and interior, but fortunately he'd stockpiled plenty of Tufftech in advance.

One of the key advantages to the new material was that, when sprayed with a chemical destabilizer, it became pliable for about half an hour, making it easy to cut and shape. Once the final form was achieved, a coat of fixative hardened it permanently.

With the main structure and shell complete, he was busy installing the motor. It would take another week's work before the craft could be flown, but Jean-Luc felt good about what he'd accomplished.

By the time he checked his watch, it was nearly noon, the time when the party was scheduled to begin. Guiltily, Jean-Luc realized he was going to be late.

In the back of the hangar, he scrubbed the oil from his face and arms as best he could and changed into a clean shirt and jeans. He wished he dared fly the bird to Newport, but with so many guests expected, there might not be room to land. Besides, he didn't want to risk having the craft dented in the crush.

Anyway, he really wasn't in a hurry to get there. Parties had never been Jean-Luc's favorite scene, and despite Sandra's assurances, he doubted this one would be an exception.

Heading down the freeway in his sport-utility vehicle, he pondered again the mystery of his attraction to Sandra. It couldn't simply be a matter of her natural beauty; sexual chemistry was more complicated than that.

Why should the fluttering of her hands, a gesture he had found annoying when he saw it on television, now inspire a primitive desire to protect her? Why should her mischievous sideways glances fill him with the urge to kiss her senseless?

Today might be the cure, Jean-Luc told himself, although without much hope. Seeing Sandra in her milieu, among her socialite friends, should destroy any lingering belief that she and he could ever feel at home together.

Morning fog had kept the beach traffic light for a summer weekend, and he reached Newport in about an hour. The street leading to the beach house, however, was filled curb-to-curb with luxury cars.

Jaguars. Ferraris. A classic DeLorean. Rolls-Royces, Lexuses, Cadillacs. Despite his skepticism, Jean-Luc found himself staring at one huge, gleaming 1930s Bugatti that must be worth millions.

There was nowhere to park, and Jean-Luc was wondering how far away he needed to go as he swung past the beach house. Then he spotted one open space on the private turnaround, roped off with streamers and labeled: "Reserved for Mr. Duval."

A Strauss waltz was playing from the house, and he could hear happy shouts from the beach. Maybe this wouldn't be so bad, he thought as he parked. After all, it was hard for people to act snooty with sand in their shoes.

Jean-Luc made his way between tightly packed cars toward the house, which fluttered with colorful windsocks. The aroma of barbecuing reached him, and then he heard someone cry, "Dad! Hey, Dad!"

Chris came racing from the house with Chanel right behind. The children wore bathing suits and hats with cartoon-style rabbit ears jutting upward.

"Hi, kids." He crouched down and scooped them into his arms. Snuggling them close, Jean-Luc realized he'd hardly seen the twins this week. "Are you having a good time?"

"We've been waiting for you." Chanel spoke in her

own voice. She hadn't hidden behind Fluff Nose since the day Sandra arrived.

"Yeah, where were you?" demanded Chris. "You haven't even had any ginger ale yet."

Jean-Luc started to laugh. Who could figure kids out? For the life of him, he couldn't imagine why they were so eager for him to drink ginger ale. "Well, let's go find Sandra."

As they neared the house, he spotted a group of well-dressed people on the beach. For a minute, he couldn't figure out why they were standing around so stiffly, and then he noticed the croquet sticks.

A tall, sleek woman, whom Jean-Luc recognized as Nita Fryberg, the head of a movie studio, whacked a wooden ball. It dribbled a few inches in the sand and stopped, arousing a chorus of jovial catcalls from her fellow players. The woman grinned.

A couple of surfers in wet suits loped by, staring at the scene in disbelief. Jean-Luc knew how they felt. Among the scantily dressed sunbathers, the croquet players appeared like a tableau from another world.

With one child tugging each hand, he entered the house. The airy rooms swayed with music, and in the living room a Japanese man in a three-piece suit performed a stiffly formal waltz with a model who had graced a recent cover of *Just Us*. Two teenage sitcom stars, each wearing a portable CD player, were performing hip-hop dances to difference rhythms.

When he glanced into the dining room, he could barely see the table for all the platters of food. A buxom redhead with a baby on her hip scooped some guacamole from a bowl, tasted it and ordered a dark-haired man to add more garlic salt. The couple fit the description of Sandra's friends Belle and Darryl, but the children didn't give Jean-Luc time to stop and introduce himself.

They tugged him onward into the den. There, he found that someone had unrolled a large sheet of black plastic, marked it into squares with the help of contact paper, and turned the room into a giant checkerboard.

Party-goers wearing red or black baseball caps were the checkers. The real fun appeared to come from those who'd been stacked together on a single square, including Mrs. Octavia Smith and a rap star with braided hair.

It appeared to Jean-Luc that the two of them were holding a private rhyming contest. From the dowager's animated expression, she was having no trouble keeping pace.

"Where'd Sandra go?" Chris asked.

"She was here a minute ago." Chanel clutched Jean-Luc's hand as if afraid he would escape.

With a tightening in his throat, he realized how much he wanted to see his wife. Or stepmother, or whatever she was. He'd made a point of avoiding her all week, and now he missed her.

"I'll bet she's outside," said Chris, and out they went, plowing through the guests.

Behind the house, Jean-Luc caught sight of her near a built-in barbecue. Sandra stood between Marcie and Ruthanne, all of them shading their eyes and gazing toward the ocean.

She wore a short pink skirt and a silver stretch top that quivered every time she breathed. On her head, a sombrero dripped with beach paraphernalia: a knotted piece of driftwood, seashells, a candy-bar wrapper, a child's plastic sandal with a broken strap, and a scrunched beer can.

"It's a dolphin." Sandra pointed out to sea.

"It's a surfer," said Marcie. "He's kind of cute. Look at his rear end."

"Don't you think...I mean, the curvature...has to be a submarine, wouldn't you say?" murmured Ruthanne.

"Maybe we're being invaded," said Sandra.

"By cute surfers with tight butts?" Marcie added hopefully.

"It's a seal," Chris said in disgust. "Come on, you guys."

Three faces turned toward him, the expressions shifting from argumentative to welcoming as they caught sight of Jean-Luc.

"Hello there." Sandra's tone was sultry. How did the woman manage to make him feel as if they were alone in a boudoir, despite the surf crashing, the croquet players cheering and his entire family watching?

"Oh!" said Marcie. "Hi, Jean-Luc." She didn't look very happy to see him.

"Bad news?" He hadn't talked to her for a few days, and wasn't sure she'd had time to make any more inquiries about Rip Sneed. A private investigator had to put paying clients first, after all.

"No news, and that's bad news," sighed Marcie. "The man's given me the slip again. I'm sorry."

"It's not your fault." Jean-Luc hadn't allowed himself to dwell on what it would mean to Sandra if she was left penniless, but now he was beginning to see that she might not be so helpless after all.

Judging by the enthusiastic turnout at this party, she would quickly find some role to play among the elite of Los Angeles. Besides, she owned fifteen percent of his helicopter company. With Sam Orion's help, it might not be too long before that represented a decent amount of money.

"Oops!" Sandra hurried to flip the hamburgers on the grill. "I nearly forgot about those."

"Well-done is safest, anyway," advised Ruthanne. "Let me watch them. Honest! I like keeping busy."

"Thanks." As Marcie drifted off to check out some men playing volleyball down the beach, Sandra joined Jean-Luc and the children. "It's good to see you."

"You guys ought to dance," said Chanel.

"Should we?" Sandra raised one eyebrow at Jean-Luc. "With my stepson? Would it look right?"

"*I'm* your stepson!" retorted Chris.

"Then *we* should dance." Linking her arm through the little boy's, Sandra escorted him into the house.

Jean-Luc followed with his daughter. "May I have the honor of this dance, Chanel?"

"That's not how you're supposed to do it." A solemn little face frowned up at him. "You're supposed to dance with Sandra."

He would like nothing better. But Sandra was right. It would be impossible to put their arms around each other and sway to the music without revealing at every turn how they felt.

How they felt? And how was that? he demanded of himself with a touch of anxiety.

"Well?" said Chanel. Jean-Luc realized they had reached the living room.

Mrs. Octavia Smith, having abandoned the checkers game, was twiddling the dials on the boom box. A moment later, out burst the head-splitting rhythms of a group that almost certainly had Smashing or Crashing or Bashing as part of its name.

"That's more like it!" crowed the dowager, and began gyrating alongside the rap singer who had shared her checker space.

Pulling his daughter to a clear spot, Jean-Luc danced alongside her. Reluctantly at first, Chanel began to wiggle, then hop around. Nearby, Chris and Sandra caught hands and spun in a circle.

They were all getting out of breath when Belle came and slipped plastic stemmed glasses into their hands. "Thanks, but what's this?" Sandra asked.

"Ginger ale. I'm just following instructions." With a wink at Chanel, Belle retreated.

"You're supposed to drink it," said Chris.

"I didn't think we were supposed to pour it in our ears," Sandra answered.

Jean-Luc started to laugh. Maybe it was the raucous music or the fizz of bubbles against his palate, but he hadn't felt so carefree in a long time.

Or so close to falling in love. He wanted to swoop Sandra into his arms and fly her to the stars, and the way he felt right now, he wouldn't need a helicopter to do it.

Everything could be worked out. Everything *would* be worked out. He wondered why he'd wasted so much of his life taking a dark view of things.

Then, across the room, the sunlight reflected off a thick pair of glasses. The man ducked his head and revealed the odd-looking crewcut that Sam Orion had worn since he and Jean-Luc went to high school together.

The co-inventor of Tufftech had arrived. But from the grim expression on his face, he evidently wished that he was somewhere else.

9

SANDRA WATCHED in dismay as the joy vanished from Jean-Luc's eyes. A moment earlier, he'd resembled a kid on Christmas Day. Now, after one glimpse of Sam, he looked as if he'd just learned that there was no Santa Claus.

As he strode away, she shooed the children toward the back door. "You guys go see if Ruthanne's got your hamburgers ready."

"Why?" demanded Chris.

"Your daddy's got business to discuss," she said firmly. "And so do I."

Reluctantly, the children obeyed. Sandra's heart wrenched as she watched them go. Then, with a sense of impending doom, she went to join Jean-Luc.

He and Sam had retreated onto the blacktop, standing between cars where the other guests couldn't hear them. "I'm sorry," Sam was saying as she approached. "I really did try my best."

Jean-Luc turned toward Sandra, his violet eyes hooded. "His partners insist on auctioning the rights to the highest bidder. All the rights."

"When?" she asked.

"A week from Monday." Sam shrugged apologetically. "They couldn't see accepting shares in a helicopter company that doesn't have any capital or any immediate prospects of raising any."

"What if we found other partners?" Sandra wished she could talk privately with Jean-Luc before voicing her ideas, but Sam was edging away as if eager to leave. "There are a lot of prominent people here today. Some of them might be interested."

"No," Jean-Luc said.

"Why not?" asked his friend. "It's a reasonable idea."

"If I thought these people believed in me, that would be one thing." The words came out so taut they vibrated. "But they would only invest in my business to indulge Sandra. I'm not a charity case."

She wanted to thump his thick skull. "Once the rights are gone, it's over, Jean-Luc. Sooner or later, you'll prove this was a good investment. Why let pride get in your way?"

"Because this is who I am," he snapped. "I refused to be my father's pet poodle, and I won't be yours, either." He clamped his jaw shut as if afraid he would say too much, turned sharply and marched away down the beach.

"Oh, dear," said Sandra.

"He's always been like that." Sam blinked owlishly. "I kind of admire him."

"So do I, except that he's messing up his life." Just as he'd done before, with Malcolm, Sandra reflected. And yet she couldn't entirely blame Jean-Luc for wanting to lead his life his own way.

"I'm sorry to be the bearer of bad news," Sam said.

"Don't give up yet," she said, although she didn't have the foggiest idea of how things might be changed. "In any case, please stick around and have some food."

"I'm afraid I don't have much appetite." With an apologetic smile, Sam departed.

Leaning against a car, Sandra tried to figure out what to do next. If she had been the only person involved, she would have gone without hesitation to her guests. As far as she was concerned, this was a perfectly legitimate business opportunity, not a charity case.

But Jean-Luc didn't feel that way, and she had no right to go behind his back. She knew instinctively that, if she did, she would alienate him just as Malcolm had.

If only there was some way to locate Rip Sneed! But at this point, even if she found him, she doubted he had any money left. What *had* he done with it all, anyway?

"It didn't work out with Sam, did it?" Marcie approached hesitantly.

"No. And Jean-Luc won't accept help from my friends."

"He always was stubborn." With a sigh, the detective pushed a wedge of dark hair behind her ear.

"Is there anywhere you haven't looked? For clues, I mean?" Sandra asked.

"Nowhere that I can think of." The violet eyes, so like her cousin's, blinked in the bright afternoon light. "Except this house. I left that to you and Jean-Luc."

Sandra felt a stir of irrational hope. "We didn't do a very thorough job. We left in kind of a hurry."

"Sneed did live here," Marcie pointed out. "On the other hand, I kind of snooped around while we were decorating this morning. Force of habit." She had arrived an hour early to help. "It's got such an open design, there aren't any real hiding places."

"Did you look behind things?" Sandra asked. "Like the refrigerator or the washer and dryer?"

Marcie nodded. "I always check there. I mean, even when I'm not supposed to."

"You mean you look behind your friends' refrigerators and washers?"

"You'd be surprised what turns up," Marcie said, as they strolled back toward the house.

"Like what?" asked Sandra. "Besides lint."

"Lost socks." Marcie grimaced. "Pieces of fossilized candy. I found a plastic bag with three baby teeth behind Jean-Luc's refrigerator once."

"That must have been a thrill."

Loud music and guests demanding attention swarmed around them as soon as they reached the front door. People wanted to set out the food and needed to know where the paper plates were, and what utensils to use, and which bowl of potato salad to uncover first. Every time Sandra turned around, someone else had a question.

Jean-Luc returned and began quietly helping to serve the food. His features were frozen into a polite mask that discouraged conversation.

Had he really given up his dream? Sandra didn't think he would yield this easily. But after so many setbacks, the shock of this latest disappointment must have numbed him.

Today was Saturday. They only had until a week from Monday to work things out. By the time he recovered his initiative, it might be too late.

For the next few hours, Sandra's brain wouldn't stop buzzing. How had Rip managed to live here without leaving any more hints about his activities? Or was she just not noticing something like a clue right in plain sight?

The food got eaten, games were played, people went swimming in their clothes and declared it a marvelous innovation, and there was much dancing and drinking of soda pop. Through it all, Jean-Luc wandered like a robot, playing the role of dutiful host without an ounce of emotion.

"He's rather cold, isn't he?" murmured Octavia as she prepared to leave. "I do think it's kind of your stepson to put you up until you get your home back, but he doesn't seem very sociable."

"He's having an off day," said Sandra. "Thanks so much for coming. And for all your help."

Ruthanne volunteered to take the children home early. They were getting cranky, perhaps because their father steadfastly refused to dance any more. For some reason, this seemed to disappoint them, particularly Chanel.

At any other time, Sandra would have tried to get to the root of the little girl's unhappiness. But today there was too much at stake, so she allowed Ruthanne to take them home.

With the crowd dwindling, she wandered back to the master bedroom and sat on Rip Sneed's former bed. Sandra closed her eyes and tried to think like a ratsoid slimeball thief.

It did no discernible good. But when her eyelids fluttered open, she found herself staring at the small bookshelf.

Why had Sneed bought a copy of the novel *Prizzi's Honor* and the script of *The Godfather*? The man seemed obsessed with the Mafia, yet Hal Smothers had assured Jean-Luc that there was no connection.

Idly, Sandra noted the other titles. *My Life in the Mafia. La Cosa Nostra. Organized Crime in America.*

She picked up the stack of scripts. Beneath *The Godfather* lay the screenplays for several other gangster-related movies, plus one with no name on the cover.

She flipped it open. Typed on the first page was the title *Mafia Odyssey,* and then "First Draft."

More from curiosity than because she expected to learn anything useful, Sandra began to read. Within a few minutes, she no longer noticed the noises from the beach or the rock music still throbbing in the living room.

She was caught up in the harsh and ungrammatical world of a small-time Mafia hitman named Vic Massey. She couldn't stop reading as the cold-blooded Massey stalked a union organizer, only to discover at the fatal moment that he had just killed his own niece.

From that point, however, the story weakened. Massey's attempts to atone for his act seemed artificial and unconvincing. She knew it was supposed to be a tragic moment when the now-reformed killer turned himself in to police, but she didn't believe in his transformation. The first part of the script had been so good that she felt let down.

Was this a true story or an invented one? And what did it have to do with Rip Sneed?

She reviewed the clues Marcie had uncovered. Sneed had paid money to several small entertainment-related firms, possibly for movie or video projects. He'd had people coming and going at his motel room, including a cameraman and several sleazy-looking women who claimed to be actresses.

He'd rented a series of storefronts. In the script, two of Massey's victims were shopkeepers.

Was it possible Sneed had invested in a legitimate production company and not some X-rated enterprise? He'd obviously been fascinated by the Mafia, so it was no wonder this script appealed to him.

But why had two rough-looking guys been searching for him in Las Vegas? Had he stolen the script, or promised more money than he could deliver? And what had happened to the film itself?

The only way to find out was to locate Sneed. It seemed unlikely that Sandra could recover her millions, but it had become a matter of pride to find out why she'd been cheated and where the money had gone.

At this point, Jean-Luc was so touchy that he might nix the whole idea. It would be better not to mention it to him, she decided. That way she avoided open conflict.

The tricky part, of course, was how to succeed where Marcie had failed. Pressing her lips together, Sandra stared out the window as if seeking inspiration.

On the beach, the croquet game had long ago been abandoned. An assortment of lingering guests, including a couple of editors from *Just Us,* had thrown caution to the winds and were playing in the sand, building a castle.

It was a huge sprawling thing with turrets and towers, and onlookers had gathered to stare. Directing the project was Nita Fryberg, who had risen from production secretary to chief of a major studio.

Several times in the past, Nita had suggested that Sandra might have a natural talent for producing and should take classes in the subject. She'd never been interested enough to follow up on that advice, but Nita had remained a friend, as demonstrated by her attendance at this party.

Maybe the way to find Rip wasn't through computer records and motel registrations. If he was involved in producing a movie, someone in Hollywood—a casting director, an actor's agent, a location scout or a designer—must know where to find him.

Should Nita Fryberg put out the word that she was looking for Rip Sneed, an answer would probably come back faster than a speeding stunt man. Tucking the script beneath her arm, Sandra hurried out to have a few words with her friend.

"So what if the ginger ale didn't work," Chanel said. "We can always try something else."

Chris made a face. They were sitting on the floor of their bedroom with stuffed animals piled around them like a fort. "That was a disaster. Dad's really mad at us."

"We didn't do anything wrong."

"Then why's he so grumpy?" demanded her brother.

The last two days had been miserable. Dad had spent Sunday pacing around the apartment like a lion in a cage. Then this morning he'd gone off to the garage with a hard, mad look, as if he couldn't bear returning to the place.

Sandra seemed kind of twitchy today, too. She'd decided to reorganize the kitchen, and had taken out all the pots and pans and moved them around three or four times.

Every time the phone rang, she jumped, and then when it turned out to be nothing important, she went back to clanging the pots and pans. Once she dropped the entire silverware drawer with a bang that made Chanel wet her pants.

"Maybe he's grumpy because there were too many people at the party," she said.

"No, there weren't." After a moment, Chris added, "Too many for what?"

"For falling in love." She scrunched her nose as she tried to remember what she'd seen in movies. "Those stories where people are dancing, they kind of end up alone. On a patio in the moonlight or something, where they can kiss."

"Then what happens?"

"Then they wake up in bed together."

"Daddy and Sandra always wake up in bed together," Chris pointed out.

"No, they don't. Not anymore." Here was a complication that Chanel hadn't considered. "Not since he bought the sleeping bag."

"I think it's neat. I wish he'd let me use it."

They stopped at a tap on their door, which was followed by Sandra's face peering into the room. Reorganizing the kitchen had left her hair tangled and a streak of dirt on one cheek. "I have to go downstairs to get the laundry. Would you kids listen for the phone?"

"Does that mean you want us to answer it?" Chris asked.

"That's the general idea."

"Dad never lets us."

Sandra sighed. "On second thought, it's a portable phone. I'll take it with me."

Chanel jumped to her feet. "I'll help you."

Her twin kicked her in the ankle. "What're you, crazy? You hate doing laundry."

Chanel drew herself up until she felt tall and adult. "Shut up," she said, and followed Sandra out.

Anybody but her brother could see that Sandra was expecting an important call. Chanel was determined to find out what it was.

They were in the laundry room folding towels when the phone rang. Sandra stuck the receiver to her ear and said "Hello?" while it rang again, then remembered to punch the button and repeated, "Hello?"

She was really nervous. This must be something big.

With the phone tight against her ear, she listened for a while, and then gave an excited hop. "Oh, Nita, you're wonderful! Really? In L.A.? But did you find out what...

No, no, that's okay.'' After another minute, she said, ''Sure. I'll hang loose until I hear from you.''

When she punched the button to hang up, she was quivering like a cat ready to pounce. ''What was that?'' asked Chanel.

''Just some grown-up stuff,'' said Sandra.

The little girl frowned as she wound a pair of socks together. She'd eavesdropped enough to know that her father was trying to find a bad man who'd stolen some money. When he did, Sandra was going back to live in her own house.

''Are you going to call Daddy?'' she asked.

''What?'' Sandra dropped the T-shirt she was holding and had to shake it out again.

''Aren't you going to tell him you've found the bad man?'' said Chanel.

''We haven't exactly found him. I mean, I don't have the address yet.'' Sandra waited, as if she was making up her mind about something. ''I think you and Chris and I need to have a little talk.''

''Okay.''

They went upstairs with the laundry. In the living room, Chris was so fascinated he even helped sort his own socks while they listened to Sandra.

She explained that the runaway lawyer was in Los Angeles. By the end of the day, her friend might even have his address.

''We still don't know exactly what he did with my money,'' Sandra said. ''So I'm going to go and find out.''

''You and Dad?'' asked Chanel.

Sandra pressed her lips together while she figured out how to reply. ''I'm not sure he'd approve of my asking my friend to help. Your dad likes to do things his own way.''

"Yeah, tell me about it," Chris grumbled.

Sandra laughed as she creased a pair of jeans. "All parents like to do things their own way." Then she got serious again. "But this is different. He might get mad if he knew I went behind his back."

"But he'll be happy when you find this guy, won't he?" Chanel asked.

Instead of answering, their stepmother lifted a pair of Chris's Winnie-the-Pooh underpants into the light and turned them at an angle. "I don't understand why your underwear has a pinkish cast. Is that the trend these days?"

"It didn't used to be pink," said Chris.

A guilty look flashed across Sandra's face. Reaching into the laundry basket, she fished out a red towel. "Hadn't this been washed before?"

"I think it's new," said Chanel.

Sandra sighed. "You don't really mind pink underwear, do you?"

Chris shrugged. "I guess not. Nobody sees it, anyway."

It was time to get back to important matters. "So when are you going to catch this bad man?" Chanel asked.

"Tomorrow, I hope," Sandra said. "Now, what would you guys like for lunch?"

After she went to fix macaroni-and-cheese, Chanel tugged her brother into their bedroom. "We've got to act fast!" she said.

"Why?"

How could he be so dense? "Because when she finds this man, she's leaving. We have to make her and Dad fall in love tonight!"

"That's crazy. We already tried your idea and it didn't work."

"They need to be alone." Chanel could see where she'd gone wrong before. "Like have a romantic dinner together. Without us."

"Where will we be?"

That was when the brilliant idea struck. "Downstairs at Ruthanne's," said Chanel. "And get this! We'll take the sleeping bag!"

Her brother didn't look impressed. In fact, he looked confused. "But we always sleep on the couch when we're there."

"Well, this time we insist on the sleeping bag!" she said. "That way Dad has to sleep with Sandra."

Chris grunted. "No, he doesn't. He could sleep in our beds."

"Oh, honestly!" Chanel made a clucking noise. "They're too short. Besides, I never saw a movie where the people wake up in bunk beds. Come on, let's go get Ruthanne to help."

Chris sniffed the aroma of macaroni and cheese. "After lunch."

Chanel gave in. But she was already planning what Ruthanne could cook for Sandra and Dad's romantic dinner: bean-and-cheese burritos and some canned corn and heat-and-serve rolls.

Add a few candles, and it would be as good as the movies.

BY THE TIME Jean-Luc got home, he was tired of being mad at the world. He would sell the damn prototypes to whoever purchased the rights to Tufftech, and that would be the end of it.

Then he would come up with some other invention. It might not be as exciting as the helicopters, but in the meantime, at least he had the garage to support his family.

Not Sandra, though; not in the manner to which she was accustomed. She'd been a good sport, but he couldn't expect her to live a lower-middle-class existence forever. It had become obvious at the party that she still had plenty of influential friends and the ability to make her own way in the world.

Jean-Luc refused to dwell on how much he was going to miss her. They'd made a bargain, and she'd kept her part of it. He didn't intend to be a sore loser.

There would never be a woman like her in his life again. He'd believed once that he was in love with Nora, but he could see now that he'd been infatuated with an image, mostly of his own projecting.

Sandra was different. She was funny and bold, capable and spontaneous, warmhearted and tough. Whenever she entered a room, it was as if someone had turned on the lights.

He trudged up the stairs to the apartment, trying to frame what he was going to say. As he opened the door, he waited for the accustomed rush of children, but they failed to materialize. Then he noticed that the kitchen table had been brought into the living room and set with a cloth and a pair of candles in saucers.

"In here!" Sandra called from the kitchen.

"Are we expecting company?" Jean-Luc sauntered toward her. Then he got a good look at what she was wearing.

She'd put on the gold-sequinned 1920s gown, with a black turban wrapped around her head. Draping herself against a chipped counter, she posed with a golden fountain pen in her hand, in the manner of a cigarette holder.

"Make sure you remember the details so you can tell

Chanel.'' Sandra's eyes danced with mischief. ''She insisted on this outfit.''

''Is this some kind of a play you and the kids are putting on?'' Jean-Luc hazarded.

''Beats me.'' Sandra dropped her pose and punched some buttons on the microwave. ''Whatever it is, Ruthanne's part of it. The kids selected the menu and she fixed the dinner. They're staying over at her place, in your sleeping bag.''

''I hope this isn't what I think it is.'' Jean-Luc couldn't believe Ruthanne would be party to trying to throw him and Sandra into each other's arms. Surely his neighbor didn't believe that one night together would convince the star of Los Angeles society to spend the rest of her life in a two-bedroom apartment.

''It's kind of sweet, don't you think?'' Sandra thrust a basket of rolls in his direction. ''I guess this is the first course. Or maybe I am.''

He was trying to frame an equally flippant reply, but the words wouldn't take shape. Something about the way the golden fabric molded itself to Sandra's figure was interfering with his rational thought processes.

''Isn't that uncomfortably tight?'' he asked.

''No, it's stretchy.'' She was lifting a ceramic bowl of corn out of the microwave when she caught his gaze. He could have sworn he saw a small tremor run through her. ''Would you rather I took it off? It never occurred to me that this dress might have some special meaning for you and Nora.''

''Nothing about Nora has any meaning for me.'' He couldn't seem to stop himself from moving toward her. ''That dress never existed until you put it on. How do you get into that thing, by the way? It looks like it's sprayed on.''

"There's a zipper in the back." Sandra's breath caught as she set the bowl aside.

Jean-Luc stopped only inches away. He knew it would be the most natural thing in the world to take her into his arms and unfasten that zipper. He couldn't think about anything but the way she smelled, like a bouquet of spring flowers, or the soft, rounded swell of her breasts just beneath the clinging fabric.

From the way her lips parted and her eyes brightened, he knew she was having the same reaction. They were both grown-ups. Why shouldn't they act on their impulses?

He swallowed hard. If he made love to Sandra, he wouldn't just want her for one night, or one week. And he knew he couldn't keep her.

"Maybe—" His throat got stuck, and he had to clear it before he could continue. "Maybe we should eat."

Disappointment touched her face, only to vanish so quickly he wasn't sure he'd really seen it. "Sure."

He ached to grasp her hips and pull her close. Instead, Jean-Luc grabbed the bowl of corn and carried it into the other room.

10

WHAT HAD JUST passed between them in the kitchen?
Sandra asked herself that question as she ate a burrito
without tasting it, which wasn't easy.

She could have sworn Jean-Luc had wanted her in the
most intensely masculine way. And she'd wanted him
with a surge of feminine heat that astounded her.

Was this why the books and movies made such a big
deal out of sex? She'd never understood it when she was
married to Malcolm. Basically, she'd figured the scripts
were written by adolescent males with overactive imag-
inations.

Thinking about scripts reminded her of the one she'd
found at the beach house, and how it had led her to discover Sneed's whereabouts. Nita had called just an hour
ago with an address, which Sandra would check out tomorrow.

She supposed she ought to tell Jean-Luc. Maybe later.
Right now, she didn't want to spoil what was left of their
mood.

The irony was that she'd attended many a dinner party
with French cuisine, crystal candelabras and tuxedo-clad
string quartets. They'd never come close to being as romantic as this evening patched together courtesy of two
six-year-olds.

The room was quiet and intimate. Through the partly
open curtains, she had an unspoiled view of the star-

spangled sky, as long as she didn't look down toward the parking lot.

On the table, two stubby candles set on mismatched saucers cast a pool of light across Jean-Luc's face. His eyes burned a deep purple, and his high cheekbones cast dangerous shadows. His gaze kept searing her, and then pulling away, and then returning.

She remembered how he'd stalked her in the kitchen with that delicious sense of menace teetering on the edge of wantonness. She'd found herself hoping he would take her up on the offer of removing the dress, right then and there.

What harm could it do to explore these unfamiliar sensations with Jean-Luc? Surely once in her life she had a right to burst into flames and self-destruct.

A low sigh made her realize he must be thinking along the same lines. Then he grabbed his plate and carried it into the kitchen, leaving a void in his place.

"What's for dessert?" he called, his voice rough with frustration.

"They forgot about dessert," she responded.

"The kids forgot about dessert?" He reappeared in the doorway. "Are they ill?"

"They didn't forget about their own dessert, just ours." She piled her plate atop the serving dishes and went into the kitchen.

The harsh, overhead light did nothing to restore her mood. That, she supposed, was all to the good.

Jean-Luc pulled a box of fudge mix from a cabinet. "Then let's make some."

Sandra regarded the box in wonder. "We can actually do that? Without melting chocolate squares in a double boiler?"

"You haven't cooked in a long time, have you?" he observed as he switched on the oven.

"My mother used to make fudge," Sandra admitted. "I never did. Bad for the figure."

"You worry about things like that?" he asked as he got out a bowl and some utensils.

"Like what?" She simply couldn't concentrate, not with his firm, taut body moving past her toward the refrigerator. This kitchen was much too small for two people, unless they planned to do something licentious.

"Weight," he said.

"I am waiting," she said.

He stopped with an egg in one hand and a spatula in the other. "For what?"

"This." She stood on tiptoe and zeroed in on his mouth. Her lips grazed his, and she came closer, into his warmth, and tasted him. It was a small movement, hardly even sexual, but a firestorm raged along Sandra's breasts and shot up her thighs and made her shockingly aware of just how much more she wanted.

Jean-Luc shuddered but remained still. "We shouldn't start what we can't finish."

She managed a small pout before retreating. "It was fun while it lasted."

Swiveling, he smashed the egg against the rim of the bowl so hard he annihilated the shell. Fortunately, most of the contents fell where they were supposed to.

Sandra watched his back, fascinated by the way his muscles shifted beneath the shirt as he stirred the mix and added water. She knew what his back looked like stripped to the skin, from that day at the garage. She wanted to strip him again.

Good manners required, however, that she honor his

decision not to pursue the matter. With a keen sense of loss, she backed further away.

He was stirring so hard tiny specks of chocolate powder misted the air. Sandra inhaled the aroma. She had never associated it with other sensations before, but tonight everything blended together: her desire for Jean-Luc, the aroma of chocolate fudge, the scent of wax from the candles in the other room.

If they did it on the kitchen floor, would it count? She supposed that would depend on who was counting.

He turned toward her, lifting a wooden spoon coated with batter. "It's got raw egg in it. Want to live dangerously?"

She sneaked forward and took a lick. He gave her a crooked smile and nibbled at the spoon. He was taking more than his share, Sandra decided, and leaned forward to get some more.

Their mouths met at the spoon. Fudge streaked his hand and she could feel something gooey sticking to her cheek. Then she found his mouth against hers and his arm catching her waist, and her hands gripped his unyielding buttocks.

Somehow the spoon ended up on the counter, and he was eating fudge from her cheek, and she was unbuttoning his shirt. It happened too fast, but she wanted him so badly, Sandra didn't know how to slow down.

A groan arose from Jean-Luc as he lifted his head to gaze at her. "There's so much we haven't resolved."

"Who cares?" she said.

As if he felt the need to pour everything out before proceeding, he blurted, "I'm going to sell the helicopters to whoever buys the rights to Tufftech. I'm getting on with my life, Sandra. Can you accept me that way?"

"You can't sell them." She didn't want to talk about

this now, but heaven forbid Jean-Luc should do something foolish and irrevocable tomorrow while she was off buttonholing Rip. "Don't give up yet."

His mouth tightened. "That's what matters to you, isn't it? Getting the money back."

"The helicopters are your dream." Surely he knew her well enough to understand that she wasn't a gold digger. Or was that still what he believed? "At least, that's what I thought."

He pulled away, and cold air rushed in. Sandra felt goose bumps sprout along her arms.

"I'm selling them," he said. "Maybe it's time you stopped picturing me as Malcolm Duval's wealthy son and stomached the fact that I'm a guy who runs a car-repair shop."

"Which one of us is having trouble with that picture?" she demanded. "It isn't me, Jean-Luc."

"Well, it certainly isn't me." He opened the oven and shoved the fudge inside.

She knew the man was angry and disappointed about his invention, but he had no right to blame her. As for his assumption that she only cared about the money, it hurt more than she could express.

Maybe that had been true of her, or at least partly true, when they first met. She enjoyed being rich. But it wasn't a matter of greed or envy or social climbing.

Twelve years ago, Sandra had gone in the blink of an eye from near-poverty to wealth beyond her dreams. With millions at her disposal, fantasies came true, reality took a powder and she no longer had to bother about the tedious details of daily living.

A person could get used to that kind of life and never look back. But that was before she'd experienced a man like Jean-Luc. Without realizing it, her priorities had changed, but how could she make him understand that?

The trouble was that they didn't really know each other. They'd never had a chance to develop trust or closeness. And now it was all backfiring.

Sadly, Sandra went to change into jeans and a blouse. For now, she decided, the best she could do was to keep her part of the bargain. She would recover whatever she could from Sneed, or at least get some answers. If there was any money left, she would give Jean-Luc half.

Whether he chose to spend it on helicopters or something else was up to him.

MEDIEVAL TORTURE chambers, Jean-Luc had once read, came equipped with racks, whips and iron cages. If the jailers had also devised a lumpy couch, their collection would have been complete.

Even worse were the dreams. Sandra, blond and sensuous in a glittery dress, undulated before him. Her lips whispered sweet nothings and her fingers beckoned. But Jean-Luc was flying a helicopter and every time he leaned toward her, they made a swoop that threatened to dash them into the side of a mountain.

He woke up in a mood so foul that he avoided speaking to Sandra for fear he would further damage their relationship. That was, assuming they still had a relationship.

Last night had left him with the impression that she'd rejected the possibility of living without the hope of vast wealth. She'd vehemently opposed selling his prototypes, hadn't she?

But whenever Jean-Luc tried to pin down exactly what she'd said or what her attitude had been, he couldn't. The memory of her standing on tiptoe and kissing him blotted out everything else.

He was so distracted that he ate fudge for breakfast, which made his stomach churn. Then he reached work before he realized he hadn't stopped downstairs to check on the children.

Over the next few hours, he forced himself to concentrate on spark plugs and fan belts, because carelessness around automobiles was a good way to get hurt. He tried not to think about the anger mixed with sadness in Sandra's eyes last night, or about the new helicopter sitting nearly finished in the hangar next door.

It was around eleven o'clock when the phone rang for the third time. He'd been letting the answering machine pick it up, but either there were a lot of people who needed to talk to him, or someone had urgent business.

Wiping his hands on a rag, Jean-Luc grabbed the phone. "Duval Automotive."

"Jean-Luc! Thank goodness!" It was Ruthanne. "I've been trying to reach you all morning."

Fear hit him like a thunderbolt. The kids. He hadn't even looked in on them. "Is somebody sick?"

"No, but you may be when you hear this," said his neighbor. "I found out why Chanel was so eager...you know. To get you and Sandra together."

"Why is that?"

"Apparently Sandra found that man. Rip Sneed. This morning, before I knew about it, she borrowed my car and... Well, she said she was going on an errand. I think she went to see him."

Jean-Luc experienced a flare of bitterness at the discovery that money meant so much to Sandra that she would take off after Rip at the first opportunity. But mostly he felt concern. "Where'd she go?"

"Somewhere in L.A." Ruthanne sighed. "Chanel wanted...she said she wanted you two to fall in love. She didn't want Sandra to leave after she caught 'that bad man.' That's how I found out, you know, about Sneed."

He wondered how Sandra had done it. Maybe she'd gotten one of her friends to hire a private detective. But it didn't matter now.

The woman he loved might be in danger. He had to find out where she'd gone.

"Put my daughter on the phone," he said.

A moment later, a squeaky voice said, "Hi, Daddy." Under stress, the little girl had reverted to hiding behind Fluff Nose.

"Hi, sweetheart," he said. "Listen, I need to find Sandra."

"She said you'd be mad."

"Is that why she didn't tell me?"

"She said you like to do things your own way," piped the dinosaur. "Are you mad, Daddy?"

Mad, and worried, and wishing he could kick himself for being so stiff-necked. No wonder Sandra had gone off by herself, the way he'd angrily rejected any suggestion of help. He would never forgive himself if she got hurt. "No, honey. But you need to help me find her. Who told her where the bad man is?"

"A friend of hers. I think her name is Nita."

Nita Fryberg? He'd seen the studio executive at the beach party, but what did she have to do with Rip Sneed?

Then he understood. Sandra must have decided to track him through the film community.

It was a terrific idea. If he hadn't been so stubbornly insistent on doing everything his own way, he might have tried that route himself, instead of putting the whole burden on Marcie.

"Thanks, honey," he said. "Listen, tell Ruthanne I'll call when I find her, okay?"

"I love you, Daddy," she said.

His heart melted. "I love you, too. And Chris."

"And Fluff Nose?"

"And Fluff Nose."

Jean-Luc grabbed a sheet of paper, scribbled Closed Due to Family Emergency on it, and stuck it on the garage door. Inside, he juggled the telephone, a bar of soap and a change of clothing as he called Nita's studio and argued his way through an army of underlings until he got her on the line.

"It never occurred to me she'd go there alone," Nita admitted as she gave him the address. "Let me know what happens, okay?"

"You bet. And thanks."

The location was, not surprisingly, a motel. It was located in a seedy section of East L.A, not the sort of neighborhood that a woman like Sandra should be driving around alone.

And she was going after a man who had everything to lose. He'd already robbed her. What else was he capable of?

It would take over an hour to get there by car. At midday on a Tuesday, the traffic shouldn't be heavy, but there was always the chance of an accident fouling things up.

He had to get there fast. That meant flying the MiniCopter.

Under ordinary circumstances, Jean-Luc wouldn't have risked taking his prototype into a bad neighborhood. But these circumstances weren't ordinary.

Thank goodness he'd equipped the chopper with a

computerized map of the Los Angeles basin. It would enable him to pinpoint the motel from the air.

Hurriedly, he rolled the bird out of the hangar and got it airborne. Pushing to well over one hundred miles per hour and taking a direct route, he could be there in less than twenty minutes.

He was following the 91 Freeway due west when it occurred to Jean-Luc that he hadn't brought a weapon. He just hoped he wouldn't need one.

THE SMALL STORE across the street from the motel bore a sign: Groceries—Lottery Tickets—Beer. Iron grillwork guarded the windows and the facade was covered with graffiti.

Flanking the store sat two aging houses, also with grill-work on the windows. Their front yards had been land-scaped with rusting cars and old tires.

Sandra counted three potholes on her way into the parking lot of the horseshoe-shaped motel. These raised from Ruthanne's sedan a cacophony of bangs, creaks and groans.

How ironic that Rip had embezzled fifty-three million dollars only to end up in a place like this. She might have felt sorry for him, if it hadn't been *her* fifty-three million dollars. Now she'd been forced to drive to this same seedy motel, and in a borrowed car, no less.

Grimly, Sandra parked in front of Room 4. She considered fetching a wrench from the trunk but decided that, if she were forced to murder the little creep, she didn't want the act to appear premeditated.

It was her intention to rap lightly on the door. But some primitive instinct seized Sandra as she approached, and before she knew it she was pounding away and screaming, "Get out here, Rip! Come out before I drag you out!"

Surprisingly, no windows popped open in adjacent units and no one appeared from the manager's office to check out the ruckus. Shouted threats of bodily harm must be par for the course in this dump.

From inside the unit, she heard a scurrying noise that sounded like rats running for cover. Or, more likely, one great, big bald rat.

A scraping noise informed her that someone must be opening a rear window. Rip was escaping!

Without stopping to think, Sandra threw her weight against the door. It bounced but didn't give.

Where would he go? He couldn't flee very far without his car, and surely he must have left it nearby. But where? Her sedan was the only vehicle directly in front of his unit.

Marcie had mentioned thugs coming after him in Las Vegas. Rip must have prepared for a hasty retreat by parking in a less obvious spot. Behind the unit? If so, he'd be starting the engine any minute now.

She pounded on the door once more. Her efforts had no noticeable effect, except, finally, to bring a woman out of the unit beside it. "Hey! What's going on?"

"Hi! I'm Sandra Duval!" She clasped the woman's hand as if they were old friends and shook it firmly. "Would you mind terribly if I cut through your room? I'm trying to catch the man who stole my money!"

"Uh...oh, you're the lady on the news!" said the woman. "Go ahead."

Sandra raced into the unit. In the double bed, a dark-haired man gasped and dived under the covers. The place smelled like sweat socks and dust, but, miraculously, someone had left the rear window open.

The screen sagged. One good push and it parted company with the frame. "Sorry about that," Sandra called as she flung one leg over the sill. "Send me the bill, would you?"

"I hope you get your money back!" cried the woman. "Go get him!"

Feeling grateful that she'd worn a pantsuit, Sandra dropped into the service alley. The narrow graveled passage, which ran between the motel and a cinder-block wall, might be wide enough for a vehicle to pass but there was no space for parking.

A crunching noise drew her attention to the right, in time to see a roly-poly figure vanish around the corner of the building. "Wait!" A burst of adrenaline powered her after him.

She cornered and saw Rip's rotund body waddling at full speed toward a van parked on the street. If he got away this time, she doubted she'd ever catch him again.

Thanks to her fury and the regular sessions she put in at the gym, she was gaining on her target, but he had almost reached the van. Sandra scooped up a handful of gravel and flung it at Rip.

"Ow!" At the sidewalk, he swung to face her, his thick brows beetling together like two centipedes trying to make love. "Stop that!"

"You stop!" she yelled.

With a snort of defiance or maybe fear, Rip hustled around the van. She could hear the clink of keys as he unlocked the driver's door. Even as she ran around the back, Sandra knew she couldn't get there quickly enough.

She reached the driver's door and jerked as hard as she could, to no effect. The engine sputtered to life—and then died. For once, luck was one her side.

The motor whirred again, then subsided to a faint

clicking. Inside, Rip burst into a torrent of curse words, which were nearly lost beneath her own shouts to come out and face her like a man.

It was hard to believe that she, Sandra Duval of the Music Center breakfasts and charity balls, was howling like a banshee in the middle of a street in East L.A. But this was also the same woman who, given an unwanted kiss by a boy in junior high school, had chased him down the hall and whacked him with her backpack until he begged for mercy.

Inside the van, Rip subsided and sat staring out the windshield. They were at a standoff.

That was when she noticed a pair of rough-looking men approaching along the sidewalk. They were huge, like two of the San Gabriel mountains out for a stroll.

Inside the van, Rip must have twisted the key again, because she heard a *put-put-put* noise. Then there was nothing but his heavy breathing, alternating rhythmically with her own.

Rip was locked safely inside. She was standing out here with two broken-nosed, bad-complexioned thugs bearing down on her.

Sandra sidled around the front of the van. Maybe the men didn't want her. Maybe they were just after Rip.

No such luck. "Mrs. Duval?" growled one of the mammoths. "We've been looking for you."

"You owe us money," snarled the other.

"I've never seen you before," she said as they parted company and advanced, one on either side of the van.

"That's not the point. You owe us." They kept coming.

Sandra gauged her chances of making it back to the alley. Nil. Besides, what good would it do to disappear behind a building with these two goons right behind her?

For the first time that day, she felt a quiver of real fear. They were closing in on her. What did they plan to do, snatch her purse? Turn her upside down and shake out her pockets?

She didn't intend to stick around and find out. With a lunge born of desperation, Sandra stampeded toward Ruthanne's car. Maybe she could get inside and run them over. But the men were gaining, her ankles hurt and the breath squeezed painfully inside her chest.

At first, the buzzing overhead failed to register. When it did, it sounded like a Mercedes swooping from the heavens, and then suddenly it was there in the parking lot, rotors whirling.

Jean-Luc had come to the rescue.

11

CUTTING THE MOTOR, Jean-Luc sprang from the Mini-Copter onto the pavement. Sandra doubted that any conquering hero had ever looked so dashing.

"I've called for the police," he announced to the two startled thugs. "But if you'd like to mix it up with someone your own size, you can try me."

He wasn't actually their own size, at least not when it came to sheer bulk, Sandra thought, and he was outnumbered. But she was here to help.

And so, surprisingly, was Rip. He'd climbed out of the van and come up behind her pursuers.

"This is my fault," he said. "I can't let Sandra get hurt because of me."

"It's a little late to discover you have a conscience," she snapped.

One of the thugs held up his hands placatingly. "We weren't gonna hurt anybody. We're actors. This guy owes us money and we thought he was working for you, Mrs. Duval."

"Not in this lifetime!" she said.

Rip let out a resigned breath. "Come inside and I'll make out a check. I'm down to my last million and I'm trying to conserve it."

"Down to *my* last million, you mean," Sandra muttered, but she didn't intend to stand here and argue.

Mostly, she wanted to retreat to the shelter of Jean-Luc's arms, and that was what she did.

He pulled her close, but she could feel him glowering over her head at the other men.

"Look, mister," one of them said, "How about calling off the cops?"

"I lied," Jean-Luc said. "I didn't spot you guys till the last minute."

If he hadn't even stopped to call the police, he really had put himself in jeopardy. Sandra felt a wave of regret at not trusting him more.

"How did you find me?" she asked as they went into the motel with Rip and the actors.

"I called your friend Nita." Inside the room, he stared around. "This is amazing."

The tiny space was jam-packed with electronic equipment. Sandra couldn't identify all of it, but there was a synthesizer that must have cost a fortune, and enough film-editing equipment to launch her own studio.

Wonderful. Maybe she could take Nita's advice and become a producer, after all. At least she had the gear, thanks to Sneed.

He wrote out checks for the actors, who thanked him, apologized again and departed. Then Rip handed Sandra the checkbook and the key to the room.

"I guess all this is yours now," he said. "I'm really sorry Mrs. Du—"

He stopped, staring at Jean-Luc as if he'd just recognized him. "Oops," he said.

"Remember me?" Jean-Luc said. "The guy you managed to cut out of my father's will so thoroughly that Sandra couldn't give me a plugged nickel if she wanted to?"

"Uh, how did you get involved with this?" stammered Rip.

"We're married." There was no point in keeping the secret any longer, Sandra decided. It was sure to come out sometime. "What's mine is also half his."

The last bit of wind went out of the lawyer and he collapsed into a chair. "What are you going to do to me?"

"First we want an explanation." Only when Sandra lowered herself onto the edge of the bed did she realize how exhausted she was. Her legs ached and her hands were raw from pounding on doors. "I found a screenplay at the beach house, something about the Mafia. Were you making a movie?"

Rip nodded dully.

"Who wrote the script?"

Wordlessly, he pointed at himself.

For the first time since she'd learned of his betrayal, Sandra felt a twinge of respect for the man. The writing had been powerful and absorbing. Maybe the guy actually had some talent—or maybe this was another trick.

"How do I know you didn't steal it?" she asked.

Rip drew himself up indignantly. "I registered three drafts with the Writers' Guild. You can check for yourself."

"You've been planning this for a long time, haven't you?" Jean-Luc said coldly.

Rip gazed at him with droopy sadness. "It's been my dream to make this movie. I thought I could do it on a low budget, but I couldn't. Or maybe I'm just too weak to resist temptation. With all that money passing through my hands, how could I settle for poor-quality lighting and cheesy sets?"

"How long has this been going on?" Sandra demanded.

"Seven years."

She gasped. "You didn't even wait until Malcolm was cold in his grave!"

Rip fiddled nervously with the switch on a machine. Fortunately, the power was off. "I always intended to repay it. I figured you'd never miss a few hundred thousand dollars, and then I'd turn a profit and replace the money."

"A few hundred thousand would never have been enough to make a movie." Jean-Luc stood with arms folded, glaring down at the attorney.

"Okay, a couple of million," Rip said. "But the costs kept multiplying. It was partly Malcolm's fault!"

"Oh?" Sandra was beginning to suspect the man's inventiveness in justifying himself surpassed even his creativity as a screenwriter.

"I asked him to invest in the production, but he wouldn't," Rip said. "Because I had to do it piecemeal, it took so long that I lost my leading actor. I had to reshoot everything, and that cost a bundle."

"And before you knew it, you'd embezzled more than you could possibly repay," Sandra finished for him.

Rip hung his head. "It became an obsession. I wanted authentic locations. I insisted on ideal lighting, on getting the perfect shot. I did multiple retakes of every scene."

For most purposes, fifty million dollars would be an overwhelming amount. But even without a big-name star, it could easily take that much to film and edit a movie, especially when you had to reshoot parts of it.

"I don't suppose you've finished it," said Jean-Luc.

The lawyer peered at them hopefully from beneath his heavy brows. "I do have a rough cut."

"But you can't get a distributor because you're on the lam," Sandra guessed.

"Actually…" Rip scraped the toe of his shoe across the meager carpet. "I screened it for a distributor, but he said it's not commercial enough. Don't get me wrong! It's great! A couple of film festivals are interested and I think I could get showings in art houses."

"You'd barely break even on your duplication and distribution costs," Sandra said. "I'd never get my money back."

His shoulders sagged. "Sorry."

"Well." She gazed around the room. "Where is it?"

"Where's what?"

"The rough cut."

"And the original footage. And all the outtakes," added Jean-Luc.

"I've got a copy of the rough cut here." Rip produced a videocassette. "The other stuff is in storage. Temperature-controlled."

Sandra stared at him. Rip began to fidget. Finally he reached into his pocket and pulled out a ring of keys. "Here." He gave her a slip of paper as well. "There's the address where it's stashed. The van's yours too, I guess. But what are you going to do with my movie? You can't just throw it away!"

"I'll tell you after I watch it." She regarded his array of equipment. The motel came with a cloudy-looking TV set, and she supposed it would be possible to watch the thing here. But she couldn't get the full effect on video.

"Jean-Luc, can we use your helicopter?" she asked.

"Of course." He regarded her quizzically. "Where are we going?"

"To my screening room, of course," said Sandra.

IT HAD BEEN YEARS since Jean-Luc visited his father's mansion in Bel-Air. He'd never expected to go there again, and certainly not in his own helicopter.

Sandra said little during the short flight except for making a brief cellular call to reassure Ruthanne. Rip clung to his seat while his face turned picturesque shades of green.

He did babble once about having taken helicopter shots of a scene in Honduras. Then he'd spent the rest of the day throwing up.

As they approached the rear lawn, Jean-Luc surveyed the sprawling house, the pool and pool house and the sweeping driveway for any sign of guards. He was surprised not to spot any.

"I told you, Darryl's lawyer put everything on hold," Sandra told him. "They've probably got my regular security service making patrols."

"What about motion sensors?" Jean-Luc kept his eyes on the emerald patch toward which they were descending.

"Something was always setting off false alarms, so I had them taken out," she said. "There are perimeter sensors in the house, but I can deactivate them. It would be easier if Alice was here, but they've sent her home." She glared at Rip, who cringed. He seemed to have a talent for groveling.

Jean-Luc wondered what Sandra had in mind as far as the film was concerned. Even though she'd liked the script, he found it hard to believe Rip had created anything more than a travesty best seen on late-night television hosted by a woman in a fright wig.

They landed with scarcely a bump. No alarms went off and no guards raced toward them with bayonets.

He and Rip trailed Sandra toward the house. Afternoon

sun glorified the rose garden and the spray of orange-and-purple birds-of-paradise by the pool.

She unlocked the rear French doors, then punched a code into the security box. "They didn't change it, thank goodness."

Rip clucked his tongue. "As a lawyer, I would have advised them..."

With an effort, Jean-Luc refrained from shaking the little man. "I wouldn't be offering anyone legal advice, if I were you."

Rip fell silent.

Inside, Sandra led the way through one vast room after another. Although he'd lived here during his teen years, Jean-Luc scarcely recognized the place. For one thing, it had been redecorated. For another, he'd always regarded it as little more than a way station.

As they marched past oversize couches and exquisite paintings, wet bars and sculptures and banks of multipaned windows, he was surprised to realize that he felt no resentment. He had expected that he would, after living for so long in a tiny apartment.

Maybe his boyish resentment had faded as he came to see that he was at least half-responsible for his estrangement from his father. But also, he discovered, a palace like this simply transcended comparisons.

You could tuck a middle-class home in a corner and never notice it. There were so many bathrooms, he wondered if anyone kept count. The kitchen, glimpsed through a doorway, had enough steel counters and islands to service a hotel. The scale of the place was so vast that it seemed more of a showplace than a home.

One great chamber opened into another until at last they came to the screening room. A half dozen banked rows of swivel chairs faced a huge built-in TV screen that could be covered by a regular projection screen as desired.

"Anyone hungry?" Sandra popped behind a concession-style refreshment stand. "I could make popcorn." He heard a refrigerator door open beneath the counter. "Oh, good, there are soft drinks and a nice stash of candy bars."

He hadn't eaten lunch, Jean-Luc realized. "I'll take a chocolate bar."

"Ditto," said Rip.

A few minutes later, they settled down to watch the rough cut. Without professional titles or a finished sound track, it felt at first as if they were seeing a home movie.

"The score is completed; it just needs to be edited for the final mix," Rip assured them. "I hired this terrific composer from Slovakia, and we did the recording in France. You wouldn't believe the orchestra he put together!"

"I'd believe it," Sandra said grimly. "Not to mention what you spent on it."

"Maybe we'd better not go into that," mumbled the lawyer.

After that, Jean-Luc forgot where he was or who he was sitting with. The downward spiral of cold-blooded killer Vic Massey, the shocking moment when he realized he had killed his own niece, and his stumbling attempts to recoup his humanity were riveting.

Only the ending left him dissatisfied. Vic's decision to turn himself in to the police didn't seem wrenching enough.

The last bleak image faded. There were no closing credits and no music to soften the blow.

"Well?" demanded Rip as Sandra flicked on the lights. "What do you think?"

"It has potential," she said, "but it needs a final twist."

The bald man sat up indignantly. "Surely you're not suggesting a happy ending!"

"He needs to make more of a sacrifice when he surrenders," she said.

"More than giving up his freedom?" Rip was clearly offended that anyone would dare to criticize his masterpiece. "Possibly even his life?"

Suddenly Jean-Luc knew what the film needed. "He's just awakened to his own human potential, and we need to see that. He needs to fall in love, so that when he goes to prison, he's abandoning the only thing that's ever meant anything to him."

Sandra clasped her hands together. "It's perfect!"

"It's not perfect, it's sappy!" Rip scowled at them.

"Far from it. You want a transformation? Well, love changes the way you view the world." Jean-Luc swiveled to meet the lawyer's gaze. "It lifts you above yourself and puts everything into a new perspective."

"That's right!" Sandra said. "Suppose your hero finally experiences a selfless emotion. He loves a woman who needs him—maybe she's facing a serious illness, and he wants to be there for her. But she's gone on the lam with him, and she can't get the medical care she needs unless he turns himself in."

The resentment vanished from Rip's face. "In dramatic terms, that might work." Apparently the concept of love was foreign to him, but he recognized an effective plot device. "I shot some scenes involving Vic's girlfriend, but I didn't use them because I didn't see where they fit. I could write a few more scenes and get the same actors back."

"You wouldn't need any expensive special effects,"

Sandra pointed out. "They'd be intimate scenes, so you could shoot them at low cost."

The lawyer nodded excitedly. "I could write it to fit in with what I've already got. It just might work."

"There's a little problem here," Jean-Luc said.

The other two turned toward him, question marks in their eyes.

"Can we trust you?" he said. "How do we know you wouldn't run off again with whatever of Sandra's property you can get your hands on?"

Rip clasped his hands over his heart. "This film is my baby! My true love! I'd do anything to save it! All I ask—I beg you—is that you don't turn it over to someone else. Let me finish it."

Sandra leaned on the arm of her chair, her delicate chin resting on the palm of one hand. "You said I've got a million dollars left. I'd have to stake the whole thing on the reshoot. But you know, why not? It may be the best investment I ever make."

Jean-Luc wasn't so sure about that. Still, her friend Nita would want to see the rough cut out of curiosity, if nothing else. If she liked it, they might get a distribution deal.

But that possibility lay in the future. Right now, he had to deal with the realization he'd made when he discovered that Sandra was missing and possibly in danger. He'd been pushing it away all day, but it must be faced.

He'd fallen in love with her. It went against their bargain, and it defied common sense to think they could build a future together.

But as he'd told Rip, love changed the way a person saw the world. Right now, Jean-Luc's world was spinning all the way off its orbit.

THERE WASN'T a moment to spare the rest of the afternoon and evening. By nightfall, Sneed's equipment, score and film were locked away at the studio and Nita Fryberg had promised to view the tape that night.

Sandra was almost certain the lawyer wouldn't take off again. He had too much to gain by sticking around, and the likelihood of her bringing criminal charges would diminish greatly if he delivered a salable film.

Nita had agreed to meet with Sandra and Jean-Luc first thing in the morning to announce whether her studio would distribute the film. At Sandra's suggestion, Jean-Luc had called Sam Orion, and, based on this new information, he'd persuaded his partners to reserve the helicopter rights to Tufftech.

Yet her husband showed little reaction to the good news. Perhaps he simply couldn't believe it yet.

She hoped he wasn't angry at her for taking matters into her own hands. The worst thing that could happen, right when they were on the point of winning the day, would be to lose Jean-Luc's friendship.

But he didn't seem resentful, just distracted. She hoped it was one of those moods that would be forgotten by tomorrow.

Ruthanne had agreed there was no point in their returning to Corona when they had to be in town so early. They would stay over at the mansion, and Sandra would finally get to wear some of her old clothes. She'd kept several of Malcolm's suits for sentimental reasons, so Jean-Luc could also dress in style.

"You don't suppose the bank will haul us off to jail in our underwear for trespassing, do you?" he inquired as they ate a late-night snack in the kitchen. The housekeeper hadn't had time to dispose of any but the most perishable foods, fortunately for them, since they'd missed dinner as well as lunch.

"I'm hoping they'll be reasonable," Sandra said. "Rip promised me a complete accounting of where everything went, and what is owed to whom. He borrowed against the house, obviously, but a lot of what he spent was from the sale of things I owned outright, like stock in your father's company, so at least I don't have to repay anybody."

"You lost your controlling interest in Dad's company?" Jean-Luc said.

"Are you saying you would care?" Sandra replied, hoping for a clue to what the man was thinking.

He shrugged. "If all goes well, I'll have my own company soon. I just hate to see you deprived of your inheritance."

"Mostly I want to keep the magazine and the house," she said. Then something occurred to her that she'd missed, in all the excitement. "Do you know what today is?"

"What?" Jean-Luc downed the last slice of melted Brie on a cracker.

"It's our anniversary," Sandra said. "We've been married exactly one week!"

He grinned for the first time that day. "Got any champagne?"

"Tons," she said.

They fetched a bottle from the climate-controlled cellar. It seemed too unromantic to drink it in the kitchen, so they went outside by the pool to enjoy the balmy evening.

Overhead, the stars danced and flirted. The buildings and the estate's high fences blocked out the rest of the world, so it seemed as if she and Jean-Luc reigned over their own private planet, lords of all they surveyed.

Come to think of it, from the time she'd married Malcolm, the house had always been full of servants who knew things that she didn't and performed tasks that she couldn't. Now, when she no longer owned the place, it felt more hers than ever before.

Beside her, Jean-Luc lay stretched out on a chaise. The moonlight turned his eyes to silver and the sculpted hardness of his body into a classic Greek statue.

One thing she had always admired about ancient Greek statues was that they didn't wear clothes. "Want to go skinny-dipping?" Sandra asked.

He turned, startled. "Are you serious?"

His question forced her back to reality. "No, I guess not. But we could put on swimsuits."

"I doubt the bank left the pool heater on. We'll freeze."

She made a face at him. "You're the most unromantic man I've ever met!"

One eyebrow quirked, or at least she thought it did. It was hard to tell in the dim light. "Oh, I can be very romantic. What about my little speech to Rip on the redemptive power of love?"

"Mere words," she said.

"Do you know the code to the pool house?"

"Of course." She opened the doors and turned off the alarm. Jean-Luc scooted inside and disappeared into the dim recesses.

Soft music with a Latin beat began to play through hidden speakers. Sandra didn't recognize the melody, but it made her body sway. When Jean-Luc returned, she asked, "Are we going to dance?"

"Just come inside," he said.

Puzzled, she complied. The lounge area of the pool house was larger than the entire apartment in Corona, with a wet bar on one side and, in the center, a huge sofa that curved around a glass table. In the soft light from a recessed fixture, she saw that he had pushed aside one section of the couch and was dragging the table away to clear the carpet.

Sandra hoped he was creating a dance floor. She wanted an excuse to slip her arms around his shoulders. She ached to inhale the tang of aftershave mixed with motor oil and rest her head on his shoulder. After tomorrow, who knew whether they'd ever again be alone together?

"Lie there." He pointed at the carpet.

She bit back the impulse to tell him that, if he was trying to be romantic, he was doing a lousy job of it. "Well, since you put it so nicely, all right."

She kicked off her shoes and stretched out, cupping her hands behind her head and staring at the high ceiling. One of Malcolm's decorators had proposed having it painted with Renaissance-style angels. She had been replaced rather swiftly by someone who favored a textured paint job.

The light dimmed. A low hum began and suddenly the ceiling was transformed into pinpoints of light and swirling colored clouds, a celestial vista far more dynamic than the real night sky.

To one side, a star exploded, while the music segued into a faster Latin rhythm. Waves of color rippled outwards, making the cosmos quiver.

"What is this?" she asked as Jean-Luc stretched beside her on the floor.

"Something I invented in high school," he said. "I call it an astral projector. Dad failed to see the use of it."

"What *is* the use of it?" she asked as a flurry of scarlet comets streaked across the sky.

"It was great for getting girls to make out," Jean-Luc murmured.

Sandra began to laugh. The chuckle ended abruptly when he raised himself on one elbow and his mouth covered hers.

As his tongue parted her lips and his hand began stroking her shoulder, she decided that this might indeed be the man's greatest invention.

12

FOR SO LONG, Sandra had held back from touching and stroking and tasting Jean-Luc that she hardly knew where to begin. But she didn't need to make conscious decisions; her body was making them for her.

Their mouths connected with such startling intimacy that she felt as if they had completed a circuit. Electricity flowed between them.

Jean-Luc arched over her, one hand stroking her blouse upward from her pants. His warm breath tickled across her bare stomach.

Yielding to temptation, Sandra cupped his hips with her hands, enjoying the tight muscles of his buttocks. The man was impossibly well-built, and absolutely delicious.

This, she realized, was how a woman was supposed to feel about the man she loved. She was supposed to relish his restrained power and to be seized by a primitive driving need of her own.

Sexual desire was the one thing her marriage had lacked. Now that she had found it, she intended to savor every minute.

Jean-Luc smoothed the blouse up around her shoulders and loosened her bra. Cool evening air teased her nipples, only to be erased a moment later by his hot, moist tongue.

Sandra gasped as he gently compressed her breasts, bringing the peaks together where he could suck each in turn. Channels of fire flashed through her body until her blood turned molten.

Somehow she managed to unbutton his shirt. The rubbing of his bare chest against hers heightened her sensitivity until she felt as if they might both fly through the room like comets.

Whatever was going on overhead had nothing on what she was experiencing. Even the slightly rough pressure of his cheek against hers roused her to new and almost unbearable heights of longing.

With swift, sure motions, Jean-Luc eased off her slacks and panties. Her vulnerability delighted her. With anguished anticipation, she leaned upward and ran her tongue down the line from his throat to his stomach, as far as she could reach.

A wild, hoarse sound tore from his throat. It almost alarmed Sandra until she realized she had unchained a part of the man he had locked away for too long.

She wanted that part of him. She want to entice it and enrage it almost beyond endurance and then satisfy it so completely there would be nothing left but stardust.

Jean-Luc's ability to control himself, even now, impressed her. She would have to congratulate him later, if she remembered. But somehow Sandra doubted it would seem important.

Certainly not as important as getting his belt unbuckled. "Darn this thing," he muttered as he struggled with it.

"Let me help." She sat up.

"Well, sure." With a grin, he half rose over her and braced himself against the couch while she worked on the stiff leather and the defiant metal prong. Gradually she got them loose, and completed the task by unhooking and unzipping his pants.

That was when Sandra found herself face to face, so to speak, with the most tantalizing and erotic portion of the male anatomy. She had never felt much curiosity about that particular organ until now, certainly not a wish to get up close and personal with one.

But Jean-Luc's was impressive. And for tonight, it was hers to explore.

Carefully, almost reverently, she ran her palms along both sides of it. Overhead, she could hear his rapid intake of breath.

Sandra feathered her fingers along the skin beneath his shaft, and was rewarded with a gasp. Then she did something she wouldn't have believed she would ever consider doing. She leaned closer and took him into her mouth.

The moans racking Jean-Luc were all the encouragement she needed. Acting on pure instinct, Sandra began moving her lips up and down. Her man's guttural noises deepened into gruff cries.

She felt as if she held his essence inside her. In the ability to excite Jean-Luc, she found both power and, in a way, submission.

With infinite reluctance, he drew himself away. "Let's not rush things," he choked out.

"Oh, let's do," said Sandra.

He gazed at her in the faint light with an expression of wonder. The next thing she knew, she lay on the carpet and he was stroking her thighs apart.

Now it was Jean-Luc's turn to tantalize, but Sandra didn't need much encouragement. She wanted that hard part of him inside her with a fiery ache.

He pressed against her yielding softness, stroking her with his hardness. She heard a groan, and was amazed to note that it came from her own throat.

As if it were a signal, Jean-Luc pressed himself slowly

into her. The thick shaft came as a relief, an answer to a longing that had become almost painful.

Then he moved inside her. To Sandra, it was as if she'd never made love before. Certainly she had never experienced these rocketing thrills spreading through every vein and corpuscle.

She reached up and held his buttocks. They tightened and eased as he moved rhythmically in and out of her. "Yes," she whispered.

"I can't—wait." He kissed her and plunged into her again and again, that fierce part of his body driving out the last of her restraint. Suns exploded and meteors flamed through the heavens and Sandra felt grateful just to have lived long enough to discover that the world contained such pleasure.

And then there was more, a great volcanic burst of joy and hunger. She could have sworn she had melted right into Jean-Luc.

The sensations faded gradually. They lay in each other's arms, touching from knee to hip to shoulder, neither willing to move until at last the cool night air drove them to get dressed and adjourn to the bedroom.

JEAN-LUC AWOKE in a rich swathe of sunlight. He blinked, registering a profound sense of physical well-being combined with a hint of disorientation.

The bedroom was enormous, a bright, rambling space furnished with white-and-gold furniture. The coverings on the king-size bed glowed with the delicate colors of sunrise, picking up coordinated hues in the banks of window draperies.

In one corner, low steps descended to a nook furnished with a love seat and an entertainment center that would have sent Chris and Chanel into seventh heaven. Nearby, a curtained doorway led into a bathroom that he vaguely recalled as being of Roman dimensions.

At last he recognized the place. This had once been his parents' bedroom, but Sandra had redecorated with soft pastels and curvaceous furnishings. The canopied bed also showed a definite feminine appeal.

Beside him, the mistress of the house lay dozing, blond hair curled around her cheeks in angelic abandon. The silky comforter had slid down to reveal a bare shoulder, hinting at what lay so tantalizingly hidden beneath its folds.

She was a portrait of newly initiated innocence. That wasn't possible, of course, since she'd been married before, and yet Jean-Luc could have sworn she'd experienced something new last night. He certainly had.

He'd felt at one with her in a way that had never happened before, as if he and Sandra vibrated on the same wavelength. More than that, it had been the first time that a woman's satisfaction had meant more to him than his own.

He hadn't realized it until now, but the disappointments and struggles of the past decade had tempered him like fine steel. He had become capable of loving someone selflessly and completely, and that someone was Sandra.

He wanted to build a life together, but it was important not to overwhelm her with sudden demands. He sighed. Subtlety was not his strong point.

A small yawn drew his attention to Sandra. Her eyelashes fluttered against her cheek, and then her blue eyes flew open.

"Oh!" she said. "I wasn't dreaming. Thank goodness!"

"Want to prove it?" he teased, stroking a lock of hair

from her temple. "We could do it again and see if it seems familiar."

Her laughter danced through the air. "What a lovely idea." Then her expression sobered. "What time is it?"

He glanced at the Roman numerals on an ornate French clock beside the bed. "It's either six-thirty or seven-thirty. Why don't you get a digital clock?"

"Because I hate them." Sandra leaned across him to look. "Seven-thirty! We've got to get dressed and meet Nita at the studio by nine!"

"Plenty of time." He stretched, managing to catch her in his arms on the downstroke and press his face into her hair. She smelled of flowers with a trace of smog.

"It's hardly any time at all!" Wriggling away, she hopped out of bed. Jean-Luc rolled on his side to admire her nude figure in the morning light, but she pulled on a peignoir so fast that he scarcely got the chance. "We have to make plans for the rest of the day, too!"

"Why?" he said.

"Because there's so much to take care of!" She clucked her tongue in mock disapproval. "You do look splendid. Push the covers off your hips and give us a thrill, would you?"

"Only if you take off that bathrobe."

She shook her head. "I need to see Darryl's lawyer and make arrangements with the bank so I don't lose the magazine. Not to mention the house. And once Nita approves the distribution deal, you'll want to firm things up with Sam."

Reluctantly yielding to the inevitable, Jean-Luc got up and followed Sandra into the bathroom. "Aren't you making a big assumption about Nita?"

"She'll love the film. It's quality work, the kind that wins Academy Awards. How can she refuse?"

Now, where had she gone? He could hear her voice, but she'd vanished around one of the curved walls of the bath enclosure.

"Even so, let's not rush things." Opening a drawer, he selected one of half a dozen new toothbrushes and went to work on his teeth. "We can take it one step at a time."

The pelting noise of the shower alerted him to Sandra's whereabouts. As soon as he finished brushing, Jean-Luc rounded a corner to discover a textured glass door that provided tantalizing glimpses of her pink body as she scrubbed.

"We can't afford to delay" came her reply. "How long do you think it will take the newshounds to figure out that I'm back? After I meet with the lawyer, we'll have to call a press conference."

"Not we. You." *If* she was right about Nita, Jean-Luc wanted to get contracts drawn up for Tufftech right away. And of course he would need to return Ruthanne's car, and reassure the kids that all these changes weren't going to disrupt their lives.

If only he could be sure that was true! Sandra seemed so happy to be restored to her old life, he couldn't imagine her choosing to return to that worn, cramped apartment.

She'd seemed fond of the children, but that didn't mean she wanted to be a full-time mother. Or any kind of mother.

If Jean-Luc obeyed his instincts, he would wrench open that shower door, plunge into the spray and demand that she marry him. Or rather, stay married to him. They could announce it to the world along with everything else.

But he didn't want their future together to be one more

item on Sandra's agenda. Or another tidbit for the reporters and the public to gossip about.

And if he pushed too hard, he risked scaring her off. He certainly wouldn't have time to woo her back with reporters and film executives and lawyers buzzing around.

That didn't mean he had to slink away, though. With a smile at his own effrontery, Jean-Luc opened the shower door and stepped inside.

"Perfect timing!" Slanting him a foxy look, Sandra ducked under his arm and stepped out. "It's all yours!"

"You'll pay for this!" he yelled.

"Let's keep our fingers crossed that we'll soon be able to pay for everything!" she called back, and vanished in a cloud of steam.

"I ALWAYS SAID you had the instincts of a producer." Nita Fryberg smiled at Sandra over a cup of coffee at the studio commissary.

The plant-draped executive dining room, empty except for them, was crammed with posters of the studio's hits dating back to the 1930s. Nita had insisted they come here to eat, once she learned that Sandra and Jean-Luc hadn't taken time for breakfast.

"You liked the film?" Sandra didn't want to press her friend too hard. Despite her bravura to Jean-Luc this morning, she was far from certain that Nita's judgment would match her own.

"I hate to say it of a weasel like Rip Sneed, but the man has talent." Even while eating scrambled eggs, Nita managed to look like God's next-door neighbor. Maybe it was her power suit or the straight slash of hair across her neck, but Sandra suspected it was her height. Sitting down as well as standing, the woman towered. "The changes you suggested are right on the money."

"The love angle was mostly Jean-Luc's idea," Sandra said.

Nita quirked an eyebrow at the man sitting silently between them. "Would you be interested in coproducing?"

"Thanks, but I've got my own work cut out for me." Briefly, he sketched his plans for the MiniCopter. "If I can secure the rights, of course."

"Which brings us to money," said Nita. "You'll need an advance to get this completed and keep the wolves from the door."

"That would be nice," said Sandra.

"Of course, I'm hoping you'll sign a contract with my studio to work with us on future projects," Nita said. "We'll be making an offer to Rip as well, but I wouldn't ask you two to team up again unless you want to."

"You're going to sign Rip?" Sandra asked dubiously.

"That's great." Jean-Luc leaned forward. "Now all we have to do is garnishee his wages and he can start paying us back."

Nita released a bark of laughter. "I'll leave that to you people to work out. Anyone care for more coffee?"

As they went over the details of their arrangement, Sandra's brain whirled so fast she had to force herself to concentrate. So much was happening in such a short time.

The most important thing was that Jean-Luc would be able to afford the rights he needed to Tufftech. That was what he'd worked toward for years and why he'd agreed to help her. How wonderful that she'd been able to help him in turn.

She tried to shove personal concerns aside, but her thoughts kept returning rebelliously to last night. Who could have dreamed that a body contained so many nerve endings and that all of them could be activated at once?

It was as if Sandra had lived for thirty-two years in ignorance of her own sexuality. No, of more than that, because what had happened between them had transcended the physical.

She didn't have time to think about it now. Nita was offering her financial security on a platter, as calmly as if it were another serving of eggs. Security, not only for Sandra but for Jean-Luc and the children too.

This was no time for daydreaming. It was time for listening and negotiating and making dreams come true.

13

ON MONDAY AFTERNOON, Sandra parked the Rolls-Royce in the driveway and staggered to the porch with her arms full of scripts. She was still fumbling for her key when the housekeeper, Alice, opened the door.

"I was listening for you!" explained the housekeeper, who hadn't stopped beaming since Sandra rehired her. "I keep pinching myself to make sure you're really back."

"Oh, thank you!" Sandra said as Alice swept up the scripts and carted them away. "Just put them in my office, will you?"

"If you're hungry, I made poached salmon with capers!" came the reply. "It's in the fridge."

As soon as she was alone in the marbled entryway, Sandra began to sag. She couldn't believe how busy she'd been since last Wednesday.

As planned, she had held a press conference, which drew so much media to one of Nita's soundstages that every spare inch was festooned with wires and video equipment. Over the next few days, she had granted enough interviews and photo opportunities to satisfy the press that they knew the whole story of Sandra's disappearance—although she'd glossed over her relationship with Jean-Luc.

In view of her new contract with Nita's studio, the bank had been happy to arrange a payment schedule for the house. The magazine had been reclaimed, and she'd given the entire staff a raise. She had sent bouquets to thank Belle and Octavia for their support, and a check to repay Marcie for her time and expenses.

Rip had spent the past weekend writing new scenes, which Sandra had approved this morning. The reshoots would begin as soon as locations could be found.

Once word of the producing contract hit the news, scripts had come pouring in to be considered for her next project. Sandra had brought home enough to occupy her spare time for a week.

Then today, a clothing company had offered big bucks to attach her name to a line of fashion accessories. She would probably agree, with the provision that she have creative control over the designs.

Just thinking about it all set the adrenaline flowing. Ages ago—before last week—Sandra would have relished being the center of so much activity, and in a way she still did. But it no longer seemed like enough.

She had talked to the children twice on the phone, or, rather, to Chris and Fluff Nose. Chanel had retreated again, according to Ruthanne, and rarely spoke in her own voice.

Ruthanne had accepted Sandra's invitation to become her personal assistant in place of the perfidious Eloise. However, they'd agreed that the new job would have to wait until the children went back to school.

Now Sandra wondered what the kids were doing. She wished Chanel was here to climb onto her lap for story time, and that Chris would demand a peanut-butter sandwich with lumps in it.

Jean-Luc hadn't been home when she called; in fact, they'd hardly spoken all week. He had left telephone messages for her at the house and the studio, and she'd returned the calls to his cell phone. Each time, he'd been inspecting a potential manufacturing site or working out the contract for Tufftech, and they'd exchanged only a few superficial comments.

She knew he wasn't avoiding her. They'd both been sucked into a whirlwind, and eventually it would abate. But by then the emptiness inside her might develop into an abyss.

Retrieving the plate of cold salmon on lettuce with a side of marinated artichoke hearts, Sandra wandered out to the greenhouse room where she and Malcolm used to eat breakfast.

The hanging orchids and fuchsias, which had been watered automatically during her absence, fluttered like butterflies in a slight draft. Outside the glass walls, the rose garden shimmered in late-afternoon sunshine.

Sandra slid the plate onto a teak table and sat down to pick at her food. Where was Jean-Luc right now and what was he thinking about?

She owed him a great deal. Not just because he'd helped restore her wealth, but because he'd opened new doors in Sandra's self-awareness.

She knew now that she could adapt and cope without the protection of money. She had also discovered, much to her surprise, that she loved children.

Even more, because of Jean-Luc, she had learned how to love in a mature way that suited her adult self. Her relationship with Malcolm had been in many ways childish; he had showered her with attention and she had responded with unquestioning affection.

With Jean-Luc, she had learned that loving meant sometimes taking the initiative, and sometimes stepping back. It meant being a partner in every sense. And he had awakened in her a sexual responsiveness that gave promise of enriching her life.

Ordinarily, she wouldn't have hesitated to ask him and the children to move in with her. But the two of them had made a pact when they married, and he'd given no indication that he wanted to change the rules.

She felt honor-bound to go through with a divorce as soon as it was practical. True, they'd consummated the marriage, but they'd both known what they were doing. Now she had to let Jean-Luc go, and hope that someday he would find his way back.

Across the red-tiled floor, something black and creepy gave a hop. A shriek bolted from Sandra's lips, but she bit back the urge to follow it with a series of screams. She wasn't in need of rescuing by the housekeeper, and besides, it was only a cricket.

She scooted from the table and unlocked a glass door that led outside, then dropped her cloth napkin over the cricket so it couldn't dodge away. Scrunching her face in an expression of disgust, she took the little beastie outside and released it.

There, she had set one creature free. Didn't that cancel her obligation to be similarly noble toward Jean-Luc?

Sandra returned to her seat and attacked her salmon with new appetite. It might take weeks or months, but she was going to corner that man and do something shocking, like rip his clothes off and hide them until he agreed to love her forever.

Well, that might not be exactly the right plan, but she would mull it over until she hit on a better one.

Her spirits rising, she reached for the TV remote control. It was a few minutes past five, so there might be some news. She even dared hope that, for the first time in weeks, she wouldn't be on it.

The lead story was about the President returning from a visit abroad. Then there was coverage of a local fire, followed by a report on a group of environmental extremists who claimed redwood trees were sentient beings that communicated via their roots in a kind of Morse code.

"When we return, we'll have today's business news, including the auction of rights to a revolutionary new type of material that could change your life! Stay with us," said an anchorwoman.

Sandra's heart leaped into her throat. It had to be Tufftech. Did this mean Jean-Luc's negotiations had fallen through, or was it an auction of the other rights? Would there be any mention of his helicopter company?

She could barely endure the commercials. Finally the business reporter came on camera.

"A group of inventors today netted bids that could total more than $3.2 billion when they auctioned off a variety of rights to..." He went on to describe Tufftech, while the screen showed a plush showroom where men and women in three-piece suits held up cards to bid, while a bank of assistants took additional offers by telephone.

Sandra had once attended a sheep auction with Malcolm and a friend of his who owned a ranch in Colorado. As she recalled, the action had been fast and furious, the smell exhilaratingly noxious and the sheep a lot more interesting than these stuffy people.

It amazed her that companies with serious money would even submit to an auction. Then she remembered that the federal government sometimes auctioned rights to broadcast frequencies, so maybe it wasn't that unusual.

"But one buyer got the jump on everyone else," the announcer continued. "Before the auction began, Jean-Luc Duval, son of the late aerospace magnate Malcolm Duval, treated buyers to a demonstration of just what can be done with Tufftech."

The hum of a smooth-running engine filled the room and the camera cut to a parking lot. As men and women in suits stood around shading their eyes, the MiniCopter glided from the sky into a perfect landing. The rotor retracted, and it taxied along one lane until it stopped inside a car-sized parking space.

"How'd you like to own one of those, folks?" asked the reporter. "That would sure cut the morning commute!"

What Sandra couldn't understand was why the station didn't shut off the whirr of the helicopter motor, even after the anchorpeople returned. Rather than diminishing, the noise was getting louder.

It sounded as if a luxury car, or several luxury cars, were descending into her back yard. Then she realized that the sound wasn't issuing from the TV set.

Through the glass wall, she saw the MiniCopter and its not-quite-identical twin lower themselves in tandem. Between them was stretched a banner that read: "We Love You, Sandra."

She couldn't decide whether to scoot back her chair or push the table away, so she jumped to her feet and knocked everything over. Out the door she ran without even stopping to clear the mess.

In front of her, the two birds settled onto the lawn. Inside one, she recognized Sam and Ruthanne. From the other peered two tiny faces, noses flattened against the glass like waifs peering into a lighted window on Christmas.

Behind the controls sat Jean-Luc. His dark head was turned partly away as he finished switching off the chopper, and the slanting sunlight carved deep hollows on his cheeks.

The doors flew open and the children pelted toward her. Sandra was nearly bowled over as Chris and Chanel hurled themselves into her arms.

The next few minutes passed in a blur as she greeted Ruthanne and Sam, while Jean-Luc busied himself checking over the two MiniCopters. Alice came out and offered to take everyone on a tour of the house, and Sandra gratefully relinquished her guests.

After the group vanished into the mansion, a hush fell over the yard. Sandra and Jean-Luc were alone. The dark-haired man straightened beside one of the helicopters, and sunlight set his violet eyes aglow.

He came close enough that Sandra could smell his aftershave. "I found a site for—"

"I was just watching you on the—"

They both stopped. "Ladies first," said Jean-Luc.

"You found a site for your factory? Where?" Her heart was thumping so loudly, she was surprised he didn't ask what the knocking sound was. What if he intended to move to Arizona or Nevada?

"Ventura County." His mouth twisted wryly. "I could get there in fifteen minutes by air."

"From here?"

"I made a certain assumption." He stood very still, his legs braced. "About where we would live. Of course, you could say no."

"I could?"

"In which case I would buzz your house at five o'clock every morning on my way to work," he warned. "And fill the studio with so many flowers you'd get hay fever. Naturally, I'll be bringing your stepchildren—excuse me, grandchildren—to visit several times a week, which means you'll have me underfoot, too. We're family now, Sandra. I'm not going to be easy to get rid of." Then he added softly, "Unless you really want to."

Her throat was so tight, she could barely squeeze out the words. "I don't."

"You don't what?"

"Want to get rid of you."

The tension eased from his body. "Well, that's a relief." Then he swept her into his arms so fast that Sandra's head whirled.

Or maybe she was just dizzy from the intensity of his kiss, and the tingling pressure of his body against hers. "Does this mean we're staying married?" she asked.

He lifted his head. "Only till death do us part."

"Do you think we should hold a press conference?"

He gave a shout of laughter. "Is that the only thing you can think of?"

"You know how the press gets things muddled—oh, phooey on them." Sandra's mind spilled over with plans and joyous possibilities. "I can't believe it. You'll be living here, you and the kids. I'll have Alice stock crunchy peanut butter and we'll get a safety cover for the pool and fix up the game room for the kids. And we'll stay married forever and ever."

"There's only one condition," he said as she nestled against him.

"What?"

"On my side of the bed, I want a digital clock."

"Done," said Sandra.

"And the next time I join you in the shower—"

"We stay joined," she finished as they started toward the house.

"That," he said, "sounds like as close to heaven as we're going to get in this lifetime."

It sounded that way to Sandra, too.

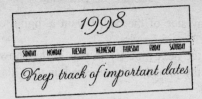

1998

SUNDAY MONDAY TUESDAY WEDNESDAY THURSDAY FRIDAY SATURDAY

Keep track of important dates

Three beautiful and colorful calendars that celebrate some of the most popular trends in America today.

Look for:

Just Babies—a 16 month calendar that features a full year of absolutely adorable babies!

1998 CALENDAR

Just Babies

16 months of adorable bundles of joy!

Hometown Quilts 1998 *Calendar*

A 16 month quilting extravaganza!

Hometown Quilts—a 16 month calendar featuring quilted art squares, plus a short history on twelve different quilt patterns.

Inspirations—a 16 month calendar with inspiring pictures and quotations.

Inspirations

A 16 month calendar that will lift your spirits and gladden your heart

Steeple Hill™

HARLEQUIN®

Value priced at $9.99 U.S./$11.99 CAN., these calendars make a perfect gift!

Available in retail outlets in August 1997.   CAL98

Take 4 bestselling love stories FREE

Plus get a FREE surprise gift!

Special Limited-time Offer

Mail to Harlequin Reader Service®

> 3010 Walden Avenue
> P.O. Box 1867
> Buffalo, N.Y. 14240-1867

YES! Please send me 4 free Harlequin Love and Laughter™ novels and my free surprise gift. Then send me 4 brand-new novels every other month, which I will receive months before they appear in bookstores. Bill me at the low price of $2.90 each plus 25¢ delivery per book and applicable sales tax if any*. That's the complete price and a savings of over 10% off the cover prices—quite a bargain! I understand that accepting the books and gift places me under no obligation ever to buy any books. I can always return a shipment and cancel at any time. Even if I never buy another book from Harlequin, the 4 free books and the surprise gift are mine to keep forever.

102 BPA A7EF

Name	(PLEASE PRINT)	
Address	Apt. No.	
City	State	Zip

Every month there's another title from one
of your favorite authors!

October 1997
Romeo in the Rain by Kasey Michaels
When Courtney Blackmun's daughter brought home Mr. Tall,
Dark and Handsome, Courtney wanted to send the young
matchmaker to her room! Of course, that meant the single
New Jersey mom would be left alone with the irresistibly
attractive Adam Richardson....

November 1997
Intrusive Man by Lass Small
Indiana's Hannah Calhoun had enough on her hands taking
care of her young son, and the last thing she needed was a
man complicating things—especially Max Simmons, the
gorgeous cop who had eased himself right into her little boy's
heart...and was making his way into hers.

December 1997
Crazy Like a Fox by Anne Stuart
Moving in with her deceased husband's—*eccentric*—family
in Louisiana meant a whole new life for Margaret Jaffrey and
her nine-year-old daughter. But the beautiful young widow
soon finds herself seduced by the slower pace and the much-
too-attractive cousin-in-law, Peter Andrew Jaffrey....

**BORN IN THE USA: Love, marriage—
and the pursuit of family!**

Available at your favorite retail outlet!

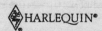 

As Seen on TV!

Free Gift Offer

With a Free Gift proof-of-purchase
from any Harlequin® book, you can receive
a beautiful cubic zirconia pendant.

This stunning marquise-shaped stone is a genuine cubic
zirconia—accented by an 18" gold tone necklace.
(Approximate retail value $19.95)

Send for yours today...
compliments of HARLEQUIN®

To receive your free gift, a cubic zirconia pendant, send us one original proof-of-
purchase, photocopies not accepted, from the back of any Harlequin Romance®,
Harlequin Presents®, Harlequin Temptation®, Harlequin Superromance®, Harlequin
Intrigue®, Harlequin American Romance®, or Harlequin Historicals® title available at
your favorite retail outlet, together with the Free Gift Certificate, plus a check or money
order for $1.65 U.S./$2.15 CAN. (do not send cash) to cover postage and handling,
payable to Harlequin Free Gift Offer. We will send you the specified gift. Allow 6 to 8
weeks for delivery. Offer good until December 31, 1997, or while quantities last. Offer
valid in the U.S. and Canada only.

Free Gift Certificate

Name: _____

Address: _____

City: _____ State/Province: _____ Zip/Postal Code: _____

Mail this certificate, one proof-of-purchase and a check or money order for postage
and handling to: HARLEQUIN FREE GIFT OFFER 1997. In the U.S.: 3010 Walden
Avenue, P.O. Box 9071, Buffalo NY 14269-9057. In Canada: P.O. Box 604, Fort Erie,
Ontario L2Z 5X3.

FREE GIFT OFFER   084-KEZ

ONE PROOF-OF-PURCHASE
To collect your fabulous FREE GIFT, a cubic zirconia pendant, you must include this
original proof-of-purchase for each gift with the properly completed Free Gift Certificate.

084-KEZR

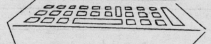